Scribe Publications
THE BLACK RUSSIAN

Lenny Bartulin is the author of *A Deadly Business* (2008). His poetry and short stories have appeared in numerous publications, including *HEAT*, *Meanjin* and *New Australian Stories*.

To Jim

Feb 2010

THE BLACK RUSSIAN

A JACK SUSKO MYSTERY

LENNY BARTULIN

Enjoy! with best wishes...

Lenny Bartulin

SCRIBE
Melbourne

Scribe Publications Pty Ltd
PO Box 523
Carlton North, Victoria, Australia 3054
Email: info@scribepub.com.au

First published by Scribe 2010

Typeset in 11.5 on 14.75 pt Dante by the publisher
Printed and bound in Australia by Griffin Press

Quote on p. 17 *From Russia with Love* by Ian Fleming
© Glidrose Productions Ltd, 1957, reprinted with permission from
Ian Fleming Publications Ltd

Quote on p. 121 *The Art of War: The Denma Translation*, translation,
essays and commentary by the Denma Translation Group, ©2001
The Denma Translation Group. Reprinted by arrangement with
Shambhala Publications Inc., Boston, MA. www.shambhala.com

'If I Had Possession Over Judgement Day' on pp. 144, 145
Words and Music by Robert Johnson
Copyright © (1978), 1990, 1991 MPCA King of Spades (SESAC) and
Claud L. Johnson (SESAC), Administered by MPCA Music, LLC
All Rights Reserved

National Library of Australia
Cataloguing-in-Publication data

Bartulin, Lenny.
The Black Russian: a Jack Susko mystery.

9781921640261 (pbk.)

A823.4

www.scribepublications.com.au

To Jules

SOMETIMES, IT WAS JUST BAD LUCK. Life was a lot of walking backwards into the future, so you could expect to fall into a muddy ditch every now and then. Brush yourself off. Do what you can. But Jack Susko was beginning to feel there was probably more to it than that. He had started to look for *reasons*. He was weighing up String Theory. Because bad luck was never just simple, even if on the surface right now it looked pretty straightforward and clear.

The lady with the .38 snubnose in her hand said: 'Everybody against the back wall. But not you, Jack. You stay right there.'

Thunder and rain outside, camera flashes of lightning. Two hundred thousand dollars packed into a couple of suitcases in the corner. Ten grand stuffed down Jack's pants. Dead guy on the sofa. And the Russian, like a statue of menace, refusing to do as he was told.

'If you have a brain, *mademoiselle*,' he said, 'I suggest you use it.'

The .38 tilted up a little. 'Don't think I won't do it, Mr K.'

A moment passed by, heavy as lead. The Russian waited, but then conceded and took a small step back. The gun swung around onto Jack. 'Now,' she said. 'How about you hand that postal slip over?'

The lucky door prize that everybody wanted. It had come in the mail, all by itself, slipped under the door the other day while Jack was at work, minding his own lack of business. *Sorry we missed you. Regular Parcel. Available after 4.30 p.m.* Except that in the end there was nothing regular about it. Especially compared to the parcels that usually arrived at Susko Books. And now here he was, staring down the barrel like a big black hole.

She held out an impatient hand. 'Don't make me shoot you, Jack.'

He unbuckled the flap of his bag and reached in. Looked up from the gun into her rich brown eyes. A second slotted into place as though on the dial of a giant iron clock; then another. What the hell use was quantum physics now?

$$\sim 1 \sim$$

JACK SUSKO WAS GRATEFUL, but it was not the kind of inheritance that changed your life. Twenty-year-old, functional Japanese family sedans in light metallic blue had never been high on the list of all-time top one hundred things in the world you could inherit. Even if it came with faux-sheepskin seat covers and an interior that smelt intensely of fruits-of-the-forest, no matter how long you kept the windows open. If he was a little disappointed with Aunt Eva's generosity at the end of her life, it was that the air-conditioning did not work. And right now the radio said it was thirty-eight degrees Celsius in the city. Jack was on Oxford Street, at 4.30 p.m. on a Friday, with traffic tight and stalled behind a broken-down bus. And it had been a long day. And he was still hustling his weary trade in weary books. And he had not smoked a cigarette for almost seventeen-and-a-half hours.

To my dear nephew Jack, I leave my 1989 Toyota Camry.

The air was thick with humidity, stained with exhaust fumes. Heat rippled off every surface: even the asphalt was sweating. Drivers blasted out a Morse code of frustration with their horns and pedestrians fanned themselves with magazines and swung violently at the flies. Jack was meant to be at De Groot Galleries in Woollahra an hour ago. November was nearly over. Hopefully he would get there before Christmas.

The car was a surprise. Jack had not seen his aunt in many years, not since she used to look after him on the weekends, when he was about twelve or thirteen. He remembered that her husband had already died by then: and that she had a son called Carl. Jack used to read to her sometimes, crime novels and romance stuff, short stories out of magazines. Her eyes had gone, she said, but the truth was she liked a drink. She used to say 'Gentle this up for me, love' when she thought the ginger ale in her glass was out of proportion to the brandy. The lawyer told Jack she had died of liver failure. 'Still,' he had added, 'eighty-six ain't a bad time for it to happen.'

Aunt Eva was a Susko. With a bit of luck, alcohol tolerance was in the genes. Since giving up the tobacco, Jack had indulged a little.

The traffic started to move again. Jack crawled up the hill and finally turned into Jersey Road. Finding a park in Woollahra was the equivalent of striking oil in a pot plant. He eventually wedged the Toyota into a spot down Spicer

Street, between an arctic-white BMW 7-series and a shiny black Range Rover Sport. He hoped nobody rang the police to have the Toyota towed away as an abandoned car.

Jack slung his bag over his shoulder and walked up to the main strip. The high-quality cotton of his pale-blue shirt, the light, comfortable linen of his loose-fitting, khaki drawstring pants, and his bare feet flip-flopping in a pair of brown Havaianas did nothing to keep him cool. It was like he was wearing a wetsuit under his clothing. No doubt the brokers knew the smart money that morning was in anti-perspirant.

The plane trees along Queen Street provided some relief. Beneath their expensive shade, people were shopping and drinking lemon-flavoured mineral waters, licking gelatos and walking their panting pooches. In sunglasses alone there was about a million bucks strolling around. There seemed to be a particular way to wear them, too, with an almost blank but faintly smug expression that said: *And?* Jack was going to have to practise in front of the mirror when he got home.

De Groot Galleries was behind a large glass door and up a flight of polished timber stairs. He had to wait a moment as two yellow-vested couriers came down with a large canvas between them, sealed inside thick bubble wrap. He held the door open as the couriers grimaced and sweated and worked the angle so that they could pass through. They looked hot and irritated. Jack did not envy their career choice.

A stern voice from the top of the stairs. 'Do you know what you're doing? That's worth a lot of money.'

One of the couriers rolled his eyes. The other whispered: 'Fuck off.'

Jack looked past them, into the gallery above. The slope of the ceiling cut everything off from the waist up, but he could see a pair of black high heels, flared and sharply creased black pants, and a broad black belt with a silver buckle. Hands rested on wide hips like a couple of guns ready to be drawn. Jack waited for them to fire, but the legs walked away.

He let go of the door and started to climb the staircase. An air-conditioner thrummed somewhere: cold air poured over him and froze the sweat beading down his back. He shivered with pleasure. At the top he stepped into the gallery, a square, open space with a parquet floor, white walls and lots of lights. At the street end was a large window with a partition screen set in front of it. Paintings wrapped in plastic leaned against the walls: there were rolls of bubble wrap on the floor, tape guns and scissors and a cordless drill. On a small table in the centre of the gallery, a bunch of lilies slumped over the rim of a glass vase.

The lady in the black pants stood beside a long, steel-framed desk, in another room that made up an area off the main gallery. A step with a thick yellow safety stripe led into it. Smaller, framed paintings were in the process of being hung on the deep red walls. The woman had her back to him, leaning forward slightly. She had a mature figure and filled the black pants with middle-aged plumpness. Jack could hear pages being snapped over energetically.

'Mrs de Groot?' he said.

Just then a small, thin man walked in through a door, carrying a box. 'We're *closed*,' he said and kept walking, past Rhonda de Groot and straight over into the main gallery. He wore a tight, short-sleeved Hawaiian shirt, faded jeans and a pair of pale-blue espadrilles. Keys clipped to a belt jangled at his hip. His white sinewy arms held the box awkwardly; for a moment he looked like a kid struggling with the adult-sized world.

Jack watched him. The man put the box down beside the lilies. Straightened up, hands on hips. 'Can I help you?' he said, in a whiny and unhelpful voice.

'My name's Susko. I'm here to see Rhonda.'

'*Mrs* de Groot is extremely busy. Do you have an appointment?'

'Is that her?' Jack pointed. 'Why don't you ask?'

Before Mr Hawaii could respond, the woman by the desk turned around. She was reading something from a sheet of paper. A pair of narrow, frameless glasses rested on her nose. 'It's all right, Max,' she said. 'Mr Susko is late.'

Max gave Jack a look that said: *What a surprise.* Then he headed back into the smaller gallery room, through the doorway there, and down a narrow hallway. He took little, mincing steps, as though somebody had just poured something cold down his back.

Rhonda de Groot dropped the page she was reading onto the desk. She removed her glasses and looked up at Jack, raising her eyebrows slightly. 'Do you have it?' Her South African accent was mild but clipped enough to add a coolness to her irritated tone.

'That's why I'm here.'

'Good.' She glanced around the gallery. 'At least something has gone right today.'

Jack opened his bag and reached inside. Rhonda de Groot was taller than he had imagined, judging by her voice on the phone. Her bust strained against the buttons of her white blouse, while her thighs threatened anybody with ideas. She had short, loosely waved, dyed-blonde hair; brown, red-tinged sore-looking eyes; and a round face covered in a lot of make-up. Early fifties, at least. Beneath all the hard work there was a little natural talent left, but it was fading and Jack wondered if maybe Rhonda de Groot was sick of rouging her cheeks every morning before work.

'Is it the one I'm after?' she asked. 'I'm not interested in any other shows.'

Jack held up the catalogue. 'Art Gallery of New South Wales, February 10 to March 4, 1983.'

She held out her hand. Rhonda de Groot had rung him last Wednesday, annoyed and in a hurry. She had been on the phone all morning, she said, and nobody had been able to help. Her client was a very demanding pain in the arse. Susko Books was last on her list. Her first words were: 'I don't even know why I'm calling you.'

'Maybe you wrote it down somewhere?' Jack had replied. There was a pause, but she did not hang up. She explained what she was after. Jack told her he would see what he could do.

He rarely dealt with requests for art catalogues, but knew a collector from his days with *MacAllister's Old Books*. Ray Campbell was an art-book specialist in Victoria Street, Darlinghurst. He looked like David Niven and wore tweed suits and liked to maintain a bohemian air that was becoming more expensive since the family money had run out. Sometimes he parted with his babies when things got a little tight. Lately, he told Jack, his pants had been splitting every time he sat down. Jack knew the feeling.

The artist in question called himself Xanadu. He had achieved some level of fame in the 1960s and 1970s as a conceptual artist. The catalogue was for a retrospective show, titled *For Me to Know and For You to Find Out*. Jack had read a little of the catalogue essay, out of interest.

Xanadu's work is self-declaration, a communication through inexpressiveness, whereby all decisions are stripped of indoctrinating fabrics and freed in an unrelenting assault upon existing and not existing, upon factualised fiction and fictionalised fact. Xanadu's invisible sculptures and see-through paintings undulate in tranquillity, sensuality, panic, rage and anxiety. Works such as The Beef Machine *say it most succinctly: I am the expiring Universe.*

Jack hoped it had expired by now.

'How much?' asked Rhonda de Groot.

'One hundred and seventy-five dollars.'

'Fine.' She tossed the catalogue onto the desk. 'I'll write you a cheque.'

Jack nodded. Max walked back into the gallery. His look said: *Still here?*

'Call Mr Vanning, Max. Tell him his stupid catalogue has arrived.'

'Do I have to? I can't stand that man.'

'Yes. You have to.'

'I'm going to need a coffee first.' Max went to the desk and fished around in one of the drawers. He pulled out a ten-dollar note. 'Do you want one?'

'Skinny flat.'

Max pocketed the money.

'Nothing for me, thanks,' said Jack.

Max ignored him and walked off. Jack looked at Mrs de Groot. 'Could you make that out to cash?'

Rhonda ripped the cheque out of its leather wallet. 'Too late.'

'Oh well. There goes race four, number two. And he was called Prancing Jack.'

She handed him the cheque. 'Good day, Mr Susko.'

Jack slipped it into his wallet. Maybe the next customer he was due to visit that afternoon would offer him a glass of water.

He reached the stairs just as Max was walking back up. His face was drawn and pale and his eyes seemed to plead. Over Max's shoulder, Jack spotted three men following in single file. They all wore eye-masks. Like a bunch of Robins looking for Batman.

The one directly behind Max noticed Jack. A second later, his arm came out and pointed a gun in Jack's general direction.

'Mouth shut,' he said. 'Walk backwards.'

~2~

JACK'S STARS HAD SAID NOTHING ABOUT VENUS aligning with Mars for the first time in fifty years and him entering a whole new phase of the universe giving him hell. His week so far had more than hinted at it, but now it was official.

'Move it,' ordered the gunman.

Jack held up his palms. Stepped back slowly. The guy was tall, muscular: number two haircut, black T-shirt and jeans. The edge of his white eye-mask sparkled with diamantes, giving his heist-guy-with-a-gun look an interesting twist. As the rest of the gang came to the top of the stairs, he shoved Max into the gallery, hard. Max tried to stay on his feet but fell to the floor as his espadrilles came off and his legs scrambled beneath him as though he was on ice.

'I thought you said it was just the two of them?' The gunman scowled at Jack and then glanced back at his partners. 'Who the hell's this guy?'

Rhonda de Groot turned from the small painting she was unwrapping and saw the man standing over Max. Her jaw dropped a little, but nothing came out of her mouth. The second hood up the stairs rushed over and grabbed her by the arm.

'Nice and quiet, lady.'

'What ... what's going on? Who are you?' Rhonda's voice held firm. Shock was still a couple of seconds away from registering. Then she started blinking, as though dust had blown into her eyes. Jack knew it was the hot presence of the gun.

'Better if you don't talk.' The second hood squeezed her arm, just above the elbow. He was short with a significant weight problem, curly blonde hair lank with sweat, a blue shirt like a tent and three-quarter-length shorts baggy over hairless, ham-sized calves. Black eye-mask with silver fringing. Maybe they were off to a fancy-dress party afterwards.

'Did you hear me, Walter?' The gunman still had his weapon aimed at Jack. 'I said who the fuck is this guy?'

Fat boy Walter shrugged. 'I didn't see him go in.' The fringing on his mask glistened over his round, flushed cheeks.

'Christ.'

The third guy came over and stood with hands on hips. 'It doesn't matter now,' he said. He was about six foot and cowboy slim, wearing jeans and a tight white T-shirt. Thick leather band around his wrist, that appeared to have no other purpose than fashion. This time the eye-mask was plain and black.

'Doesn't *matter*? What if he's a fucking cop?'

'He's not a cop.'

'How the hell would you know?'

'Does he look like one?'

'Guys ... come on ...'

'Fucking amateurs.'

'You're all under arrest,' said Jack. 'For the masks.'

Slim guy walked over and shoved him in the chest. 'Back up, smart-arse.'

Jack stumbled a little, regained his balance, and then stood and stared at the man for a moment. He adjusted the bag on his shoulder.

'You deaf?'

'Come on, Shane, settle down. We haven't got time.'

'You'd better listen to Walter,' said Jack, nodding at the fat guy holding Rhonda de Groot by the arm. 'Shane, was it?' Two names out of three so far. Jack wondered if it was their first heist.

Shane puffed up his chest. 'Go on. Say something else.'

'What happened to the balaclavas?'

Behind him, the gunman said: 'Yeah, Shane. What happened to the fucking balaclavas?'

'I told you, for Christ's sake!' Shane continued to stare at Jack. 'The masks were all I could get.'

'You got them from the props cupboard, didn't you?' said Walter.

'So what?'

'Why didn't you get the big rubber masks, they were right there, second shelf —'

'Shut up.'

'Bullshit,' said the gunman. 'You're never fucking working with me again.'

Shane hung his head, hands back on his hips. 'Fine with me,' he said. Then he looked back up at Jack. '*Pascal*.'

'Why don't you just give 'em my fucking address!'

'Come on, let's just get on with it.' Walter slapped his thigh.

Shane reminded Jack of somebody. The way he stood. Kind of oily-hipped. He concentrated on the face, but could not see past the ridiculous mask. The name sort of rang a bell, too, but Jack was not so stupid as to ask if they had ever met before.

Max was still on the floor. Pascal the gunman reached down and snatched the keys off his belt. He tossed them to Shane. 'Lock the front door.' Then he kicked Max in the leg, hard. 'Get up, you ponce.'

'Leave him alone!' cried Rhonda.

Jack was starting to wonder if the hoods had the right address. 'You know there's a bank not too far up the road?'

Pascal pointed the gun at him again. 'Shut your neck.'

Jack nodded and shut it. The man obviously did not handle stress too well.

'What do you want?' Rhonda was having trouble comprehending the situation in her gallery.

Pascal kicked Max again. 'Up!'

Max groaned and dragged himself back onto his now espadrille-less feet. He walked into the smaller gallery room, head down and face still drained of colour. Jack followed, Pascal and Shane behind him. Walter held Rhonda de Groot's arm and led them into the connecting hallway.

They walked past a couple of doors. There was a kitchen on the right and then an *Exit* sign above the open door on the left, stairs descending beyond it. At the end of the corridor, a windowless room. It was long and narrow, lit by fluorescent lights on a low ceiling. Along the back wall, a white-laminated workbench: on the tiled floor, a couple of boxes, a timber packing crate full of polystyrene bubbles and two ergonomic swivel-back chairs. In the far corner, a vacuum cleaner sprawled like a sleeping drunk. And right next to it, a large dark grey safe, about hip high and a couple of feet wide. Jack could see there would be plenty of room inside for lots of valuable things. He was pretty sure the three masked men felt exactly the same way.

Pascal pointed at the safe. 'When you're ready.'

Rhonda looked at him, confused.

'Open the goddamn thing!'

'But there's nothing in it.'

The gunman slapped her across the face. 'Move it,' he said. 'Don't make me ask again.'

Rhonda put a hand to her cheek. Her eyes were wide and wet and terrified. She went over to the safe.

'Strap those two up.'

The two ergonomic chairs were pulled away from the wall. Jack was pushed down into one, Max into the other. Shane grabbed Jack's bag and dumped it on the floor. He began to twist packing tape around his arms, chest and the back of the chair.

'Nice mask,' said Jack.

Shane ignored him, concentrated on winding the tape.

'Why didn't you wear the cape?'

'Lone Ranger doesn't wear a cape.'

'You mean you're not the Scarlet Pimpernel?'

Pascal stepped over and grabbed Jack by the neck. His hand was large and dirty, like a welder's. 'One more fucking word.' He gave Jack's neck a bit of a squeeze and put the gun to his jaw and pressed the cold barrel into the skin. His breath was hot, smelt of too much coffee. Through the mask, the eyes looked bloodshot and dry. He let go.

Jack coughed, tried to swallow. The day had gone completely to shit. Maybe it was a full moon and all the nuts were out? He should have checked the calendar on the fridge. Next time he was locking himself in with Lois, his cat. They could play Scrabble until it was all over.

'Are we there yet, Mrs de Groot?' Pascal had moved down to the far end of the room and stood behind her as she turned the combination on the safe. She was fumbling the lock, missing the numbers. 'Five more seconds. Concentrate now.'

Walter picked up Jack's bag from the floor. He lifted the flap and had a good look inside. He pulled out a package and waved it around. 'What's this then?'

'A bomb,' said Jack.

The fat guy began to tear the brown paper wrapping. Jack watched his face, shining and red as a grilled chorizo. His three-quarter-length shorts hung low, pleading for a belt. The paper came off and he held up the book, turned it around so that he could read the cover. Then he smiled, broadly. *From Russia with Love*,' he said. 'The boss will love this!'

Jack closed his eyes and dropped his chin to his chest. The book was a first edition, worth a reasonable little bundle — the only little bundle Jack Susko had left in the world. Last

year a Swiss–Japanese woman had almost bought it for her
father, but it never happened. Not even after a fancy dinner,
a couple of lime-green cocktails at fifteen bucks a pop, and
a taxi back to her place. This afternoon he was hoping it
would sell. Jack's next stop after De Groot Galleries was to
have been a swish hotel in Woolloomooloo: an American
businessman wanted to see the book. Dan Osbourne, from
Detroit. He was flying out tonight and had asked Jack if he
would bring it over personally. If he was interested, Dan
said, he had plenty of cash on him. American dollars, too.
They could maybe do a deal. Jack wanted fifteen grand, but
was willing to go down a little. Looked like he was about to
go down a lot.

'I think it's an original,' said Walter. Jack squirmed as
the man licked his finger and turned some pages. They had
bound him to a chair and now they were torturing him. *The
name's Susko. James Susko.*

'Listen.' Walter pointed to the top of a page. 'This is
the first line.' He cleared his throat. *'The naked man who lay
splayed out on his face beside the swimming pool might have been
dead.'*

'Show me.' Shane reached out for the book.

'I'm having it, so don't get any ideas.'

The dust jacket was covered in protective archival plastic.
On the inside flap, Jack had placed a small, rectangular
sticker: *SUSKO BOOKS*. It was a nice, classy design, navy
blue lettering over cream, an elegant, thin border with
curved corners. Underneath, in smaller font, address and
phone number. Jack had five hundred of them printed when
he first opened. Just for the good stuff. The plan had been to
supplement the bread and butter of his general stock trade

with the odd lump-sum sale of more collectable books. All he needed to do was build up some capital from the day to day, and then speculate on the odd first edition. Everything was going just great. After a couple of years, he only had four hundred and ninety-nine stickers left.

Shane lifted his eyes up from the inside cover and stared at Jack. He passed the book back to Walter.

Jack had the funny feeling again, that he knew the guy. 'There's a discount for cash,' he said. 'But I'd need ID for cheque or credit card.'

'Sure,' said Walter, grinning. 'No worries.' He tucked the book in under his sweaty arm. 'I'll just test drive it over the weekend.'

There was the metal clunk of the safe door being unlocked.

'Good girl.' Pascal pulled Rhonda de Groot up from her crouching position in front of the safe. He nodded at his colleagues. 'Strap her up. And gag the lot of 'em.' He knelt down and reached in. When he stood up, there was something the size of a phone book in his hand, wrapped in a purple velvet cloth.

'What's that?' Rhonda stared at the object in the gunman's hand. She was frowning. 'What is it?'

'Nothing for you to worry about anymore.'

She looked over at Max, strapped and silent in his chair. 'Max? What was in the safe?'

'I ... I don't know. I've got no idea.'

'Get a fucking chair!'

Walter hurried out of the room. He came back a few moments later with a white plastic chair.

Rhonda de Groot was made to sit down and then tied

up with packing tape. 'What was in the safe?' she repeated. Pascal ignored her. Jack watched the gunman flip a corner of velvet cloth off the object in his hands. He grinned. Must have been something nice.

Shane came over, tape in hand, mouth set straight beneath his stupid mask. Jack leaned towards him a little, whispered. 'What about the Three Musketeers? Huh?'

No response. The length of tape went across Jack's mouth. Another couple of strips gagged Max and Rhonda de Groot.

The three masked men left. Jack listened to their footsteps down the hall: then heard them fade as the thieves descended the stairs and escaped into the street.

Silence filled the gallery, rippled only by the soft electric hum of air-conditioning.

Jack closed his eyes. *Conceptual art catalogues.* Never again.

~3~

FIVE HOURS LATER, JACK WAS STILL STRAPPED TO THE CHAIR. He was extremely uncomfortable. Half his body had gone to sleep and ached with air-conditioned cold. His blood was like day-old porridge in his veins and his fingers and toes felt numb and swollen. That he had tipped his chair over in a futile attempt to somehow escape, and had been lying on his side on the hard tiled floor for the last three of those five hours, had a lot to do with it.

Lots of phones had rung during their confinement: the two phones in the gallery, Max's mobile, Rhonda's mobile, and Jack's, too. He had even heard ringing from somewhere else in the building. It was like some kind of twenty-first-century techno-torture: all those people calling — *are you there? are you there?* — freedom ringing in your pocket but really a million miles away. A couple of times somebody had knocked on the heavy glass of the front door, the dull, hollow sound carrying all the way up to them in the now dark room at the end of the hallway. The thieves had conscientiously remembered to turn off the lights and lock up as they left.

For a while, at the beginning, Jack had watched Rhonda and Max looking at one another intently, trying to communicate with their eyes. Then they had twisted with anger in their chairs. And then they had groaned with mute frustration, like babies trying to be understood. Now their eyes were half-closed and red-veined, staring at nothing in the shadowed room.

The wall clock read 9.45 p.m. Sounds from the front door again: but not knocking. A key? Rhonda and Max stirred in their chairs. The front door gave a faint metal shudder and then closed with a glassy thud. Footsteps up the timber stairs. Casual, unhurried.

Rhonda and Max began making any noise they could. The light came on. Jack blinked, looked up and tried to focus through the painful brightness. Somebody walked into the room.

'Jesus Christ!'

Legs rushed past Jack on the floor. A moment later, Rhonda de Groot's voice. 'Richard! Richard!'

'Are you hurt? What the hell happened?'

The man had a strong South African accent. He tried to tear at the packing tape with his hands.

'Use the scissors, there, on the bench.'

'Who was it? What happened?'

'Three men with masks. They had a gun.' Emotion filled Rhonda's voice, a prelude to tears. 'They hit me, Richard.'

'It's all right, they've gone,' said the man soothingly. 'They're gone.'

'We have to call the police.'

Jack heard the tape around Rhonda de Groot being peeled roughly away. She stood up. There was an embrace: high-quality clothing swished smoothly.

'Help Max,' said the man, handing Rhonda the scissors. He walked over to Jack and lifted him and the chair up from the floor. 'Who's this?'

'Nobody. A second-hand bookseller. He was here when they came.' Rhonda removed the tape across Max's mouth, who instantly began to pant and cough. 'Oh God! Thank God!'

The man with the South African accent flicked a fingernail under a corner of the tape gagging Jack's mouth. His aftershave was spicy and went with his expensive dark-grey suit and manicured nails. He pinched the flap of tape between his fingers and pulled it off like a band-aid. Jack winced.

'Okay?'

'Yeah,' said Jack. 'Cheers.'

'I'm Rhonda's husband. Richard de Groot.'

'Jack Susko.'

'Max, call the police,' said Rhonda. Her authoritative tone had already returned.

'Wait.' Richard de Groot took the scissors from his wife. He stood behind Jack's chair and began to cut through the tape.

'Wait for what?'

'Tell me what happened.'

'I just told you. We were held up by masked gunmen.'

'Did they take anything?'

'Yes. They took whatever the hell it was that you had in the safe but didn't tell me about. Would you care to tell me about it now?'

Jack lifted his stiff arms, shrugged away the packing tape and stood up. His legs felt like deadwood. Everything else ached. He stretched a little, but too much air filled his head too quickly. What he needed was a very alcoholic drink. He wondered if he should ask.

'Well?' said Rhonda to her husband.

'Not now.'

'I want to know, Richard.'

Jack rubbed his numb thigh. He watched de Groot walk up to his wife. She was almost a full head taller and not a little wider and she used all the extra body to glare down at her husband. He reached out and held her by the forearm. In a flat, hard voice, he repeated: 'Not now.'

Rhonda shrugged him away, stepped back. 'I've just been hit, tied up and threatened with a gun. This is *my* gallery, Richard, and I want to know what you put in the safe! Are you involved in something again?'

The man shook his head and looked down and rubbed his forehead. There was quite a lot of it. His short, grey-flecked dark hair had not bothered to walk the extra distance over his high-domed head. He licked his fleshy lips. 'We're not calling the police.'

'Don't know about that,' said Jack, casually. 'Something of mine was taken as well.' He tapped the front pockets of his pants and remembered he had given up smoking the day before. Being strapped up had added another five cigarette-less hours to his record. It made him feel a little better.

Richard de Groot turned to Jack. He was a small man, but nuggety, probably go your nuts if push came to shove. The look on his face was just a notch below annoyed. He adjusted his shoulders a little.

'One-twenty Queen Street, isn't it?' Jack slipped the mobile out from his pocket and stared down at the keypad.

'How valuable?' asked de Groot.

Jack lifted his head. 'Excuse me?'

'What's it worth? I'm happy to compensate you for your loss.' The hard look eased and his tone warmed. He took a step towards Jack and held out his hand. 'Mr Susko, wasn't it?'

Jack nodded. He was suddenly thinking about his financial situation. Zimbabwe had nothing on him. After a moment's pause, he stretched out his arm and shook Richard de Groot's hand. It was cool and smooth and firm.

'Can I call you Jack?' said de Groot, raising his eyebrows.

'Sure you can, Richard,' replied Jack, as he shook de Groot's hand. Only moments before he had been tied up to a chair — and now he was doing business.

In truth, being strapped up for a few hours had been a momentary respite from his worries. Once the tape had been cut away they were back again, only worse. With the Fleming book gone, his muddy hole was now fifteen grand deeper. Jack had to listen to de Groot. He owed a lot of money and one of the places he owed it to was the insurance company. Nothing he owned was covered: even with the early summer heatwave, his worldly possessions were naked and shivering. He doubted the cops would drop murder cases and undercover penetrations into organised crime so they could go looking for his little James Bond novel.

'There's no need for all this to become … *complicated*,' said de Groot, letting go of Jack's hand. He raised his palms, gestured like a priest blessing his meagre flock. 'Complications are a waste of everybody's time.'

'It was a rare book, Richard. I'm not talking nine ninety-five on the discount table.'

'I'm sure we can come to some sort of understanding.'

Jack looked at Rhonda de Groot, who was staring at her husband. She had tilted a hip back against the bench and crossed her arms under her buoyant chest. Her face had lost a little of its anger, but her eyes were still narrow and threatening.

'So why no cops?' asked Jack. He nodded his head towards the safe. 'Something in there you don't want them to know about? Nuclear secrets? Plutonium?'

'Max, why don't you go and get us all some water.' Richard de Groot smiled. A deep crease appeared in each cheek like a couple of duelling scars. Max seemed relieved to be asked to leave and walked quickly into the hallway. De Groot loosened his tie.

'No big mystery,' he said, looking at his wife. 'I can't afford to lose my no-claim bonus.'

Jack smiled. 'That's good. I like that one.'

'It's the truth.'

'I have no doubt.'

'My wife's business is a small black hole, Jack. Nobody's buying art right now. We need to watch every cent.' Richard de Groot nodded at the safe. 'And some losses you need to take on the chin.'

Jack eyed Rhonda. She was still watching her husband. Jack wondered how they worked. The sly husband and his big tall wife. Both wearing pants.

'So what's the no-claim bonus worth?' asked Jack.

'Enough to not call the police.'

'Fifteen grand?'

'That's an interesting figure.'

'Too many curves, Richard?'

'No, not at all. I've always liked plump figures.' He glanced at his wife.

It had been a very warm day. The evening was continuing in the same vein. Jack looked around the room, felt Richard's and Rhonda's expectant eyes on him like two racks of heat lamps. He would have to make a decision.

'How about twenty thousand?' Richard de Groot rubbed his smooth chin.

Lately, Jack had been working on his impulsiveness. He had been focusing his consciousness on getting grounded in the present. Kick the cigarettes, improve his health. Save some money. It was a stressful time for Susko Books and Jack was willing to give many things a go. Unfortunately, a more balanced, healthy, Zen Buddhist approach to life did not really cut it as an asset with the local bank. And what Jack Susko needed was cash.

~4~

SOMEBODY HAD SIDE-SWIPED THE TOYOTA. The black plastic side mirror hung limply from the door by a thin wire, like a small, gutted marsupial. The mirror insert lay shattered on the road. There was no note with a phone number tucked in under the windscreen wipers. But what did he expect? It had been a long time since honesty was the best policy any place Jack knew.

He stood in the road and looked at the other cars parked around him: no matching scratches, just perfect, state-of-the-art automotive technology, shining under the glow of movement-sensitive security lights and an inky-blue night sky that caught the city's electricity like a stretched tarp. He wondered which wheels were de Groot's.

They were meeting tomorrow in the city, at Susko Books, at 11.00 a.m.

Jack had not agreed to anything specific — but he knew all about that kind of deal. It was a tune he had heard before, working for the likes of Ziggy Brandt. Only difference now, he was on lead trumpet instead of just carrying the gear. It had been a surprisingly easy step to take, only a small movement into the frame. He wondered if that was how Ziggy had started his career.

He kicked at the shards of mirror on the road. *Shit*. It was not like he had much choice. So they called the cops and everything was taken down into the little leather notebooks, the descriptions of the three masked men, everything they said, approximate times, names and addresses. Then off they go to investigate, find the perpetrators and Jack's book.

James Bond, was it? We'll be in touch. Yeah, right.

He unlocked the car. What did he care about de Groot's safe and whatever the hell was in it? The man did not want to call the cops. Could be a million reasons. And none of them had anything to do with Jack.

No, there was only one thing on his mind: he did not want to lose Susko Books. *No way*. Sometimes he loved it and most times it gave him grief, but he was in charge and he took responsibility. Something had to measure a man's satisfaction and worth. And even though the ruler was chipped and drew cracked lines and all the numbers had faded away, it was Jack's hand on it and he tallied the stats. Which was something: especially when there was a whole lot of not much else.

Friday night in Paddington. Crowds milled outside the pubs on Oxford Street: people laughed, yelled, hailed taxis, checked text messages on their mobile phones. Couples strode the footpaths in groups: the women scantily dressed in the evening heat, their buff men strutting a step or two ahead, eager with the sniff of sex in the air. The relief at the weekend's arrival was palpable. Stumbling-drunk dawn was still hours away. For the moment, everybody beamed fresh and happy, like extras in a shampoo commercial.

The Toyota rolled on through all the summery optimism. Jack felt a little better, cruising the evening. Maybe he would join the revellers tomorrow night for a well-earned drink, after de Groot's cash put a little bump in the middle of his mattress.

He found a parking spot just down from his apartment building in Leinster Street and squeezed the car in.

At the front entrance, he paused to check his mail. As he pushed a small key into the lock, a shadow moved along the road. He heard footsteps and turned to see. A dark figure approached.

'Jack Susko?'

The man's tone was not particularly friendly. Jack casually flipped through his mail, an assortment of bills, pizza and Thai restaurant menus, and a *Time* magazine meant for somebody else. 'Never heard of him,' he said.

The man pointed at Jack's mailbox. 'Apartment two?'

'You got the right street?'

The man laughed. 'Jack, it's me! Carl Reiss, remember?'

Jack looked up. The streetlights threw shadows over the man, but something tagged his memory. Aunt Eva's boy. Jack offered his hand. 'Cousin Carl.' They shook. 'I was sorry to hear about your mother.'

'Yeah, thanks. It was pretty tough at the end,' said Carl, tension in his voice. Then he shrugged. 'But you know. When you've got to go.'

'She was a lovely woman.' Jack felt a twist of guilt as he thought of the Toyota. 'I would have come to the funeral but I didn't know anything about it until the lawyer contacted me after.'

'Yeah,' said Carl, eyes flitting past Jack.

He doesn't believe me. Jack felt a moment's annoyance but did not pursue it. 'You doing all right?'

'Me? Oh, yeah, no problems ... well, I'm still getting used to it, you know, but life goes on.' Carl smiled at Jack: his messy teeth caught the sky's city lights and gleamed. 'Just getting on with it.'

'Come in for a drink?'

'Ah ... look, no, I can't. I'm meeting some friends out tonight.'

Jack nodded, looked his cousin up and down. Tall and wiry, a little hunched over in the shoulders. Awkward, just like he was as a kid.

'Do you live around here?' asked Jack.

'No, no, still in Mum's old place, out in Bankstown. Just in the area tonight.'

Jack recalled his aunt's house. 'Begonia Avenue.'

'Well done.' Carl paused. 'She at least left me that.'

A fruit bat flapped by overhead. Jack glanced up into the night sky but could not see anything, only the pinpricks of hazy stars. Not enough to distract him from his growing discomfort.

Carl checked his watch. 'I've been meaning to call you

ever since Mum died. Thought I'd pop in tonight, seeing as I was out here. I was just about to go when I saw the car turn into the street.'

'Yeah, I'm late,' said Jack. 'Got held up.'

'Working hard, huh?'

'Masked bandits.'

Carl laughed. 'Still the same Jack, then. You used to talk shit like that when we were kids. Always making stuff up.'

Jack frowned a little, kneaded the ache in his shoulder.

'Mum used to love it, though,' added Carl.

'Right.' And there was Jack thinking that as a young buck he had always been enigmatic, cool and mysterious, a child of few words. Just like Clint Eastwood in *For a Few Dollars More*, only without the cheroot.

Cousin Carl put his hands on his hips. He sucked his teeth and nodded down the street. 'So how's the Toyota running?'

'Like a gold Rolex.'

'Hey, it's a good car,' said Carl, mock defensive.

Jack locked the mailbox. Headlights swept over them from a passing car. Carl glanced down the street. 'Still can't believe you got it, huh?'

'It's not a Porsche, cousin.' Jack felt old irritations resurfacing.

'The old soft spot I'd say,' continued Carl. 'You used to pour her drinks any time of the day. And light her cigarettes with that Harley-Davidson Zippo she had.'

Jack remembered the lighter. An anomaly in Aunt Eva's world of doilies.

'I was never allowed to touch it,' said Carl. 'Ever.'

A couple more memories returned to Jack. 'You nearly burnt the house down once,' he said. He was careful not to say *tried to*.

'So you remember that.'

'Just now.'

'What else?'

Jack grinned, but squirmed on the inside. 'Running through the sprinklers when it was hot.' He wanted his cousin to go.

Carl tugged at his black short-sleeved shirt. 'I could do with some of that now.'

'Yeah.' Jack breathed in, nodded, let it out slowly. 'Anyway ...'

'Remember that time your old man came by? Gave you a walloping in the front yard? We all thought he was going to kill you. One of the neighbours called the cops.'

'I must have blocked it out.'

'Yeah.' Carl raised an eyebrow. 'It was pretty good of us to look after you, eh?'

Jack nodded, gave a strained smile. 'Nice to see you again, Carl. We'll catch up soon.'

'Listen, there's something else.' Carl's eyes shone like wet glass, stared hard and straight into Jack's. 'Any chance I could borrow the old bus?'

'The Toyota?'

'Yeah.'

'Well ...'

'I need a car for a couple days. Three or four, actually.'

'When?'

'I was kind of hoping *tonight*. You know what I mean?'

'Not really.'

'Look, I know it's an ask. But I need a car for work. My van's out of action and I can't afford to fix it right now and

I've got jobs on. And I'm on the ropes financially. Can you cut me a break?'

Jack shuffled the mail in his hands. He knew what those ropes felt like.

'I mean ... it *was* my mother's car,' said Carl.

A couple walked down the street holding hands, their voices happy, content. Carl turned to look at them. Jack remembered his cousin had been a quiet kid, nervous and prone to a mild stutter. Mostly grim-faced. But he had lost his old man early in life. And now his mother was dead, too. The guy was bound to be upset. How could Jack say no?

He began to thread the key to the Toyota off his key ring. 'Here,' he said.

'I really appreciate it.'

'No worries.'

Carl held out his hand. A calloused ridge ran across the base of his fingers, like maybe he spent the day hauling rope or trying to loosen rusted nuts with a spanner. Jack gave him the key, wondering what Carl did with himself.

'I'll have her back safe and sound in a few days.'

'Sure,' said Jack. They shook hands. 'See you then.'

Carl walked off down the street. Jack watched him and then waited until he heard the Toyota start up. He had half a feeling that Carl had somehow played him, but tried not to dwell on it.

Lois bounded out from the darkness of the apartment building's hallway just as Jack slotted his key into the door. She bumped his shins, miaowed, twisted between his legs and miaowed some more. She looked up, eyes wide. Jack reached down and scratched her behind the ears.

'It's been a long day, baby. Did you save me some dinner?'

Closed up all day, the apartment was hot and musty and smelt a little damp. Lois ran into the kitchen and waited beside her food bowl. Jack tossed the mail onto the coffee table, found the stereo remote and pressed play. *Mingus Ah Um*, 1959. He hit track two: 'Goodbye Pork Pie Hat.'

As the music started up he began searching under the sofa for a stray, forgotten cigarette. Even a half-smoked butt would do. But nothing. He put his head to the floor and scanned under the furniture. A couple of pens and a lot of dust. He checked the bedroom, the closet and his clothes, even the bathroom. Lois miaowed impatiently from the kitchen.

Jack opened a few more drawers and checked the bookshelves. Zero. He knew there was not a flake of tobacco anywhere in the place. He had crushed all his spares the day before, thrown out all his lighters and matches. So what the hell was he doing?

Lois miaowed from the kitchen again, eyeballing him. She had changed her style recently and it was only now as Jack watched her that he saw it. A certain brazen quality. No more Continental sophistication, rather a sultry, American confidence. Goodbye Marlene Dietrich, hello Veronica Lake.

The left ear was hanging down, shading the eye there, almost with a curl to it. She no longer walked anywhere, but glided, slinky and never in a hurry. When she offered you bourbon an hour before noon, you could be sure she had already cracked the bottle. And her new philosophy of life? Distilled to one sentence and you could read it on her face, any time of the day or night: *Hey mister, do I look like I care?*

Jack fed her and opened a bottle of wine, the last out of a case of five-dollar cleanskin cab merlots that he had picked up a week ago. Rough and full of splinters. He poured himself a glass, found a notebook and pen, grabbed a pile of bills, and then sat down in his Eames chair. As the leather creaked, he remembered the garage sale a few years ago when the guy had said: 'Seventy-five bucks. It's a good chair.' Jack had replied: 'Sure. Okay.' Maybe that had been it for lucky breaks. Could he part with it now and raise some cash? Did he have to? He listened to the music and went over his troubles. It was probably about time he appreciated the details.

Jack owed, give or take a dollar or two, about thirty-two thousand big ones. Bills, credit cards, outstanding payments, back rent, among other things. He had two dollars and forty-nine cents in the bank. To withdraw it from a teller would cost him a buck-fifty. All the financial papers warned it was not a good time to cash in your investment portfolio, so he decided to leave it.

There was ninety-three dollars and eighty-five cents in the till float at Susko Books. The business had turned over a meagre two-thirteen forty-five for the week, down nine fifty on the week before. From that, Jack had to subtract rent, electricity, repairs, stock purchases, petty cash and — now that Carl had taken the Toyota — bus fare. He did not need a calculator. He knew exactly how much he did not have.

He needed de Groot's money.

Jack dropped the notebook and bills onto the floor and picked up the *Time* magazine that had been mistakenly slipped into his mailbox. He looked at the address label: somebody called Gavin Porter.

He tore the plastic off, opened a page, slugged his wine. *Sorry Gav. I'll pay you back later.*

Along with everybody else.

~ 5 ~

Saturday morning. The city was already hot, loud and busy. Jack crossed York Street in front of the Queen Victoria Building and went down the steps to Susko Books, the basement headquarters to his global second-hand-book empire that so far was yet to open its second outlet. After last night's wine, his head felt as though somebody had replaced his brain with a small, just-boiled cannonball.

The porn shop above was still shuttered behind its bright yellow façade. Deepak, the owner, ran an office-cleaning business in the mornings and did not open up until after noon; he DJ'd on the weekends, too, and owned a share in an Indian restaurant out in Pennant Hills. The guy was relentless in his ambition to hit 'a million bucks before thirty', and had even offered to buy out Susko Books. At least now with de Groot's money on the way, Jack could tell Deepak no deal, and get back to his annual summer re-read of *Treasure Island*.

He unlocked the front door and walked into the quiet cool of shelved books, waiting to be held, read and loved. There was no air-conditioning, but with concrete floor, walls and ceiling, the place did all right during the summer. He closed the door behind him, dropped his keys, sunglasses and bag on the counter, and then slipped a CD into the stereo. *Somethin' Else* by Cannonball Adderley. He pressed play. 'Autumn Leaves' kicked in with its opening burst of brass. As Miles said hello with his trumpet, Jack switched on the lights. He decided to do a little dusting.

The morning cruised along: a few decent sales and even a good-looking girl browsing the fiction shelves for half an hour. Before she left, they had a nice chat about Virginia Woolf. Jack admitted to not having read her, saying nothing about his failed attempt at *To the Lighthouse*. He was never going anywhere that was so painful to get to again. But the girl said that he should definitely read some Virginia Woolf and Jack replied sure. He had plenty of her novels in stock. He might even start today.

Eleven a.m. came and went. Jack flipped through a few pages of *Orlando*. By 1.30 p.m., still no Richard de Groot. He tried *The Waves*, but his stream of consciousness could not detach itself from the image of a smooth personal cheque or a white envelope stuffed full of crisp hundred-dollar notes. Virginia went back on the shelf and Jack began dialling numbers.

No answer on de Groot's mobile, the call went straight through to messages.

'Hey Richard, it's Jack Susko. Maybe you forgot to come and see me. Maybe you should remember.'

Nobody was picking up at the gallery either. Jack's happy morning air was starting to go a little afternoon sour. He got the *White Pages* out from under the counter and found *de Groot*: fifteen were listed, none of whom had the initial 'R'. Jack rang them all anyway. Nothing. Just as his hangover had eased, a new pain in his head was starting to put the squeeze on. A case for the return of fine tobacco into his life was mounting and Jack had a strong feeling that the jury was not going to take too long with its final decision.

The front door opened. A tall, skinny, bearded man with long greasy hair. He was wearing an old, sleeveless white T-shirt with a few amber-coloured food stains under the neckline, and faded black jeans. No shoes. His arms were long and thin and tattooed. His sweaty feet made a wet, peeling noise as he walked over the polished concrete floor towards the counter. Jack sighed and waited for the inevitable. *I've got no bus fare, man, and I've got to get up to the Blue Mountains by tonight.* The guy had picked a bad afternoon to hustle charity at Susko Books.

'Hey,' he said, smiling.

Jack nodded. The guy's teeth reminded him to ring the dentist for a check-up.

'Yeah, look, this is probably a long shot but, um, would you by any chance have any, like, reference books on cults and religious groups, you know, stuff like that?'

The guy's voice was nervous but did not sound too crazy, despite the subject matter. Jack scratched the palm of his left hand, thinking.

'Might have,' he said.

'Oh, cool.'

Jack went over to a bookshelf and scanned the spines: St Augustine's *Confessions of a Sinner*; *A Light That Is Shining* by Harvey Gillman; Marcus J. Borg's *The Heart of Christianity*; *Joan of Arc in Her Own Words*; *Roman and European Mythologies* edited by Yves Bonnefoy; *Zen in the Art of Archery* by Eugen Herrigel; *When the Day Is Done* by Filipo de Tomasi. Many of them had been on the shelf for a while.

Jack checked the next row and found what he was looking for. He pulled out a large yellow book in floppy covers, an ugly but relatively difficult to get print-on-demand publication he had picked up at a garage sale in Gladesville a few weeks ago: *Dictionary of Sects, Heresies, Ecclesiastical Parties and Schools of Religious Thought* by John Henry Blunt. It was a cheap facsimile of the original 1874 edition, but reproduced the lovely antique typeface. Before handing it over to the guy, Jack could not resist flipping open a page and having a look. He got page 114.

COTOPITES, or COTHOPITHÆ. An African name for Circumellions. It is probably equivalent to the Latin "Agrestes", rustics or vagrants. [Isidore, *Origg.* viii. 5, 53. Honorius. Aug. *de Hæres.* 69.]

'This might be the thing.' Jack passed over the book.

The man looked through it eagerly. His eyes flicked across the small, tightly packed text. He jumped to the final pages and ran a dirty fingernail down the W's.

'Ah! The Waldensians,' he said. 'Perfect.' He read for a moment and then handed the book back to Jack. 'I'll take it.'

'Okay.' Jack checked the price that he had written in pencil on the title page. 'It's not cheap,' he said. 'Hard to get, actually.'

'Right.'

'Fifty dollars.'

'Oh. Wow.' The guy nodded and raised his eyebrows and his face grew dark with the shadows of disappointment. 'Gee.'

For some reason, just then, Jack did not want this man's money. His hip flask of *milk-of-human-kindness* was almost empty, but he gave it a shake and heard the barest of splashes. He may as well knock it off now. What the hell else was he going to do with the little that was left? He went behind the counter and slipped the book into a brown paper bag and passed it over to the skinny tall guy with no shoes. Fifty dollars was going to make about as much difference to Jack's financial woes as an ice-cube in an erupting volcano.

He combed the back of his head with a hand. 'How much you got?'

'Aw, you know, like, ten bucks.'

'That'll do.'

'You sure?'

'Yeah. It's fine.'

The guy smiled, a little confused, but nodded his head some more. 'Oh, that's so cool.' He shoved a hand into his pocket: the black jeans slipped further down his boyish hips. Then he passed over a tightly crumpled note. 'Thanks man!'

Jack watched the guy leave. Hopefully the universe had taken note of his good deed.

Richard de Groot remained incommunicado for the rest of the day. He did not come by Susko Books, or call, or text, or email. And he did not send an authorised representative around to complete the agreed arrangement with Jack. On the way home, the universe did not drop any wallets without identification or bags of untraceable drug money in Jack's path. No discarded lotto tickets with the winning numbers. Not even a packet of cigarettes. Maybe the universe had been too busy.

~6~

FROM THE STREET, *Ray Campbell Art + Books + Catalogues* looked like it had closed down some time ago. The glass panels of the shop-front window were painted a thin white and the small alcove leading to the front door was strewn with pamphlets and fliers and a couple of yellowing community newspapers, long out-of-date and unread, disturbed only by wind or the odd midnight drunk looking for a place to urinate. No indication whatsoever that inside it was more like the Reading Room at the British Library than empty, abandoned premises falling into disrepair.

Jack loved it at Ray's. He had always wanted to work for him, but Ray was less about business and more about sitting around reading — and that had always been a one-man operation. Jack had started Susko Books with the same kind of intent: though not quite with the same outcome. But what could you do? Good stock cost good money. *Ray Campbell Art + Books + Catalogues* had drawn a lot of its highly collectable, leather-bound stock from the family vault. Ray had inherited some real beauties and all he had to do was sell the odd one and he was able to easily afford a life of sitting around with the ones that were left. Jack's inheritance was mainly an album full of faded Polaroids and a bunch of unpleasant memories. And you could find that sort of thing at just about any garage sale you cared to look.

Ray Campbell was the only true eccentric Jack had ever met. With his old boss Brendan MacAllister away on a trip to New Zealand with his wife, Ray was Jack's touchstone and font of knowledge about everything that you never read in the papers. Jack was hoping he knew a little about Richard de Groot.

The Sunday afternoon heat and humidity had filled Ray's shop on Victoria Street in Darlinghurst to the brim, thickening the usual mustiness to something you could almost vacuum. Jack entered and breathed the dusty whiff of time that lingered there. The past in a thousand shades of brown. Shelves and tables full of rare first editions, one-off hand-illustrated cards, limited-edition artists books, signed catalogues, prints, paintings, etchings, photographs and sculptures. Knick-knacks all over the place like crumbs on a dining table: toy soldiers and cars, matchboxes and old postcards. The world brought in, so that Ray did not have to go out.

On the stereo, Gottschalk's 'Souvenirs d'Andalousie': bright, festive and cool.

'Raymond.'

'Ah, Jack! Good to see you, my man.'

'You look comfortable. Practising for a cruise?'

'Not practising, Jack,' said Ray, his usually pale face blushed by alcohol. '*Cruising*.'

'Of course. My mistake.'

Ray Campbell was reclined in a timber deckchair. Above his head, a red, white and blue striped shade umbrella, set on a slight angle. He sat low in the canvas seat, knees high, one long skinny leg over the other, a pale-green drink in his left hand. He wore a yellow shirt open at the neck, with white collar and cuffs, white braces over his narrow sloping shoulders, white pants, two-tone brogues and bright yellow socks.

'Oh, Jack, my lad. I have so few pleasant surprises,' he said as he began to struggle out of the chair. 'Come. Embrace me.'

Jack grinned. Ray sloshed his drink over the floor and held his arms out. They hugged, stiffly, punctuating their affection with a couple of manly backslaps. Jack did not slap too hard, though: he was surprised at how skinny and feeble Ray felt in his arms. A little more old age had crawled quietly into his friend since the last time Jack had seen him.

'Margarita?' asked Ray.

'What's happened to the single malts?'

'I'm in a Latino kind of mood. Have been all week, actually. Can't you tell by the music?' He shook a couple of imaginary maracas. 'I've just finished Bernal Diaz de Castillo's *Historia verdadera de la conquista de la Nueva España*. And I've been revisiting Lorca and Neruda. Not to mention Elizabeth Bishop, from her time in South America. She's wonderful. The best.' He bent down to the floor beside the deckchair and handed Jack a book. 'Here. Have it.'

'You don't need to give me books.'

'But I want to. Take it. It's a lovely little edition. Used to be my Uncle Pete's. I don't think he ever read it. *You* must.'

Jack thumbed the book, nodded. Then he looked up and said: 'Think you could spare some cash, too?'

Ray shook his head. 'Oh, Jack.'

'It's just been one of those months.'

'I know.' He smiled, sympathetically. 'How much?'

'Five hundred?'

'Done. Now, let's drink. I think you need a little more tequila in your mix. You sound weary, Jack. Three parts to one to one ought to be just right.' Ray walked over to the large mahogany table that served as a counter and book display. 'I'm getting very good at them, you know.'

'I have no doubt.'

'And I only started this morning.'

Jack watched Ray mix the margaritas. He put the lid on the cocktail shaker and gave it precisely five shakes. He poured the drinks and handed one to Jack.

'To solitude measured by conversation.'

'Cheers.'

'And sex, of course.' Ray walked over and eased himself down into the deckchair again. 'Incredible how even at my age the thought of it won't go away.'

Jack sat back on the edge of the table and drank. The cold lime and tequila hit was right on the money. 'You need to get out more.'

'And spoil my imagination?' Ray shook his head. 'No no no …' He sipped his own drink. 'Speaking of narrow imaginations, was the Xanadu catalogue okay?'

'Yeah, it was the right one.'

'God, Mr bloody Xanadu! Have you ever met him? Such an awful man. Such a lack of talent. Did you look at the catalogue?'

'Yep.'

'Don't get me started.'

Jack grinned, took another sip of his margarita. 'What about the de Groots? Know anything about them?'

'Well, now I know they have no taste.'

'It was for a client.'

'Good Lord. What kind of people are they dealing with?'

Jack held his glass up, watched the light shine through the margarita green. 'Me.'

'Present company excluded from my snide remark, of course.' Ray raised his eyebrows. 'Do they need another catalogue?'

'No. Something else.' Jack paused. 'We've agreed on … well, a small deal. A kind of exchange. And now the husband owes me some money and he's taking his time with the payment.'

Ray looked thoughtfully at Jack. 'Right. Interesting. Should I ask?'

'Maybe later.'

'Okay. Fine. So, you're asking does de Groot have a bad-debtor reputation? Well, I can't say I've ever heard anything like *that*.'

'Anything else?'

'I know they left South Africa in the '80s, like many others with money, and migrated to Australia. Getting out with their cash before apartheid completely crumbled.

And then I believe Richard de Groot went on making more money here.'

'Doing what?'

'Business. I have no idea. You know the amount of attention I pay the corporate world, Jack.'

'What about the gallery?'

A half-smile creased a corner of Ray's mouth. 'A compensatory gift for the wife.'

Jack paused the glass of margarita before his lips. 'Richard's a naughty boy?'

'Apparently so. Insatiable appetite for fresh *strumpet*, I am told.'

'Right.' Jack remembered Rhonda's tense, tired face, the heated air around her. 'He's an ugly little bastard,' he said. 'Must be the money.'

'There was an incident, not too long ago, in fact,' said Ray. 'The police were called to their house. She threw something, he tried to calm her down, that sort of thing. Black eyes and shattered vases. And it wasn't the first time, either.'

'A wife-beater?'

'Oh, she gives as good. Set fire to his car once, out on the street. The rumour was Russian mafia, but people know.'

'How do *you* know?'

Ray grinned. 'Did you meet Max at the gallery? He's an old Vietnam friend.'

'I see.' Jack nodded. He shuffled the information around in his head like a deck of cards, wondering what to play. Then he said: 'Tell me something. Why wouldn't you call the cops if something was stolen out of your safe?'

'Was something stolen from De Groot Galleries?'

'Between you and me.'

Ray frowned. 'Jack, you're not involved in something silly, are you?' His voice was firm, but concerned. 'I don't want to encourage anything untoward by lending you money.'

'Nothing to worry about, Ray.' Jack downed his margarita.

'I don't believe you.'

'Can you answer the question?'

The deckchair creaked as Ray adjusted himself. 'Well, the obvious conclusion is that this something that was stolen might have been a something *on the black*. Undeclared, bought for cash, that kind of thing. Although, just thinking about it, an art gallery dealing in contemporary work is less likely to have the opportunity for fudging the books.'

'Unlike you.'

'Are you insinuating that I am a tax cheat?' Ray held up his hand immediately. 'Don't answer that.' He sipped his drink. 'But yes, if you like. I do have just such an opportunity to … *forget* how much I sold something for. A contemporary art gallery, however, would want to work at lifting their artists' profile and value by, well, showing off the sales. They live and breathe hype.'

Jack remembered the gunman inspecting the object from the safe. 'But wouldn't most works be on the walls or on plinths or out the back in the storeroom?'

'Yes, but …'

'Maybe it had nothing to do with the gallery,' said Jack, more to himself.

Ray waved his free hand. 'Then it could be anything.'

Jack nodded, let out a breath.

'How do you know something was taken from the De Groot Galleries' safe?'

'Big stroke of shit luck.'

'Ah yes. We don't like those.' Ray climbed more successfully out of the deckchair. He pointed his empty glass at Jack. 'Another?'

'Thank you.' Regardless of his financial concerns and the question of Richard de Groot, the drink was relaxing the stiffness in Jack's neck and shoulders. 'Any cigarettes, Ray?' he asked.

'Alas, no. Banned by my doctor. Apparently, I possess the lungs of a willy-wagtail with asthma.'

'Nobody smokes anymore.'

'We know too much, Jack. No longer are we free to frolic behind blissful ignorance.' He shook his head. 'We now live in a world where being unhealthy is seen as a crime against humanity.'

Jack picked up a men's magazine lying on the table where Ray was making the margaritas. What to wear, where to go, who to read, what to drive, how to look. He flipped through it absently. Non-smoking, perfectly healthy, well-dressed gentlemen of the world. 'For the pictures?' he asked, turning a page.

'A customer left it behind.' Ray hammered the air for a moment with the cocktail shaker. The crushed ice sound was soothing and cool and Jack wondered if Ray had a spare deckchair. Drinking margaritas through the rest of a hot Sunday afternoon sounded like a good idea. Better than sitting around by himself, worrying.

Ray poured the drinks and passed one to Jack. 'Cheers.'

As Jack took his eyes from the magazine and turned towards the drink in Ray's hand, a face on the page he had been looking at flashed into his mind. Just a pulse of mute light, nothing more. But he glanced back down at the face. A couple of cogs in his brain shifted slightly. Teeth bit into corresponding grooves. And then as wheels turned and chains began to rattle, Jack knew that he recognised the guy. In fact, he had seen him just last Friday night: the only difference being that he was wearing a mask then instead of a suit.

'Sorry, Ray.' Jack took the margarita from him and drank the whole thing down. He passed the glass back. 'I've got to go. Have you got the *White Pages* somewhere?'

~7~

THE HOUSE WAS NUMBER 279. The façade was grimy pale blue, with patches of exhaust-grey rendering exposed here and there, as though the painter had given up before finishing the undercoat, realising nothing was going to help the place look any better. The balcony was boxed in with corrugated plastic sheeting, a little darker and dirtier than the blue of the façade, and the windows were draped with what appeared to be faded green bed sheets. They drooped awkwardly at an angle, as though the house had suffered a stroke.

Jack went through the front gate, down a short, cracked-concrete path, and up two wooden steps onto a small, creaking verandah. Weeds grew through the decking. He knocked.

A moment or two later, a voice: 'Just a minute!' It was a woman. Jack waited and then heard footsteps inside, growing louder as they approached over wooden floorboards. The door opened.

'Hi. Can I help you?'

She was tall; on the skinny side. She had short, nearly white-blonde hair, with a boyish fringe under a black beret. Dark eyebrows and dark brown eyes and a small mouth with full, red lipstick lips. Light-coloured skin with a dusting of freckles over the cheeks. A warm smile.

'Is Shane in?' asked Jack.

'Sorry, he's away,' she replied. 'Back Thursday or Friday, I think.' She was wearing a faded pink T-shirt, something written on it in black, shaped into a flattened circle: *Partido del Slumber, Sevilla 1987*. Denim cut-offs flashing a lot of slim tanned leg and a pair of scuffed red Converse sneakers on her feet with gold laces. Matching bright red handbag with a large gold clip, across her body on a long thin strap. Jack might have said university student, but she was older than that: maybe early thirties. And she had style. Jack sensed her confidence.

'Just on my way out,' she said. 'Can I help with anything? Take a message?'

Jack thought of a few messages but did not want to give the woman a bad impression. 'No, it's all right. I'll call back later.'

'Sure.' She stepped out of the house and pulled the door shut behind her. The lock snapped loudly. She presented her hand. 'I'm Kim, by the way.'

'Jack Susko.'

They shook hands. 'Kim *Archer*,' she added with a small

bow and smiled again. She moved past him and Jack followed her through the front gate. On the street, she stopped and pointed. 'I'm going that way.'

'Same.'

They began to walk. Jack caught a breath of her perfume, something floral but sophisticated: not meant for denim shorts, and yet worked perfectly on her.

'Shane's in China,' she said. 'Shooting a beer commercial.'

'Really?'

Kim noticed Jack's surprise. 'Yeah, I know. Finally got some paid work!' She brushed her fringe. 'He does try though, poor boy.'

'When did he go?'

'Last week, um … Wednesday? Thursday? What day is it today?' Kim laughed.

'Sunday.' Jack frowned, thinking.

'Are you an old friend?'

'Yeah. Sort of,' he said, wondering where Shane might actually be. 'Old flatmate. Wanted to say hello.'

'Oh, lucky you,' she joked. 'What's he done?'

'What do you mean?'

'Outstanding bills? Never returned your favourite jacket? Or did he borrow your car and get you demerit points and a speeding fine?'

Jack grinned. 'He owes you money, too, then?'

'Only two months' rent. I don't even want to talk about the phone bill.'

'Ouch.'

'Yeah, tell me about it. He's promised to square everything as soon as he gets back from China. He's on good money there, apparently. And I'm about to move out, so he knows I need it. And if he doesn't, he knows I'll kill him. Slowly.'

'Have you lived with him long?'

'About a year, thereabouts.'

'And he's still acting?'

'More like pretending. That he's an actor.' There was a flash of annoyance, but she dispelled it quickly, as if guilty for feeling it. 'Most of his work is modelling. He's good at that. Stands there, looks good, says nothing.' She smiled, turned her bright eyes to Jack. 'Did I just describe the perfect man?'

'You forgot to say *has money*.'

'Oh, poop! See, that always happens to me. I never remember everything that's on the shopping list. I always settle for flawed men and then wonder why things never last.'

'Just think of Shane next time.'

'Yeah, I should. It's just that Shane does so much thinking about Shane that I'd hate to clog the universe up with more of the same.'

'Sounds like you're looking forward to moving out.'

Kim sighed. 'Oh, he's all right. High maintenance sometimes, that's all. I told him that if he asked me whether he looked like Brad Pitt one more time, I was going to shave his eyebrows off while he was asleep.'

Jack remembered the chin dimple, blue eyes, short blonde-brown hair and the elastic of his Calvin Klein underpants always showing above a loose belt. 'Does he still know *everyone*?'

'One-point-two million people and counting. And he has to ring them all, all the time. Surely someone is going to help him crack the movie business!'

Jack wondered if last Friday night's heist was research for a role.

'Did you live with him long?' asked Kim.

'Just a couple of months, years ago. He was in between houses. Somebody recommended him to me as the perfect house guest.'

'Incorrect!'

'Very.'

A mobile phone began to ring in Kim's handbag. She stopped and fished it out. 'Sorry,' she said, checking the number on the screen. 'I just need to take this.'

'No problem.'

She pressed the mobile to her ear and started walking again. 'Hello! I'm on my way … Ten minutes … Yes … Yes! … What? … Oh, don't be so stupid …'

As Kim talked, they came to a set of lights at a crossing. Jack indicated that he was turning right. She held up her hand, nodding. Into the mobile she said: 'Hang on, babe, just a second. I've got to say goodbye to someone.' She took the phone from her ear. 'Lovely to meet you, Jack,' she said, warmly. Then she leaned across and kissed him on the cheek.

It surprised him. 'Yeah, nice to meet you, too.'

'He should be back end of the week. Feel free to pop around anytime.'

'I will. Thanks.'

'Bye!'

She walked off. The mobile returned to her ear and Jack watched Kim smile as she resumed her conversation. He heard her say: 'No, no! Just an old flatmate of Shane's …'

As he headed up the street, Jack glanced back. A couple of times. Which was a little strange, because Kim Archer was not even his type.

He walked. By the time he was nearly home, the nice feeling inspired by Kim had faded. High above, a plane had begun to draw smoky letters in the haze. Jack looked, squinting, wondering how long it would be before the sky was leased for more permanent advertising. Maybe he could take out a small corner ad for Susko Books. Something like: *For Sale. Second-hand book emporium. All reasonable offers considered. Will swap for a little peace of mind.*

~8~

Jack sat in his chair and bounced a small green rubber ball against the wall behind the counter at Susko Books. Thinking. Waiting. His head hurt with the effort. It would have been healthier if he were smoking.

Monday morning was always quiet. Jack usually caught up on his reading. He had started *Treasure Island* again, as he did every year, but not even old Robert Louis was able to distract him from his problems. He felt stalled, handbound: unable to contact Richard de Groot and unable to do anything about it.

He remained in the chair for about forty minutes, thinking up a storm and bouncing the ball. Wondering what de Groot was doing. Wondering about Shane Ferguson. He tried *Treasure Island* again.

My curiosity, in a sense, was stronger than my fear; for I could not remain where I was ...

The door to Susko Books swung open.

'Jack, how are you? Sorry I'm late.' It was Richard de Groot.

Jack barely recognised him. He tossed his book onto the counter and stood up. Came around, slowly. De Groot was wearing a blue cap that said *Kentucky Wildcats* across the front, and a pale-pink Ralph Lauren polo shirt with the collar up. Three-quarter-length bright white shorts. Brown, soft-leather moccasins, tan-studio legs, no socks. There was a loose-fitting gold watch on his wrist that looked like it told the time simultaneously in three different galaxies. Regulation, rich-man-off-duty style. The kind that said: *I look funny because I normally wear a suit*. He stepped down into the shop and walked towards the counter.

'Hello Richard,' said Jack. 'Not working today?'

De Groot ignored him. He stopped and put his hands on his hips. His eyes narrowed as he looked around. Short man with the big attitude. Then he glanced back over his shoulder towards the front door and nodded.

Through the glass, Jack saw another man. This guy was big: his chest looked like a retaining wall, his shoulders broad enough for children to ski on. He was wearing a light grey suit and a white tie. Everything *tight*. Buzz-cut blonde hair and sunglasses: perfectly still, just staring into the shop. He held the wrist of his left hand with his right, casually resting the grip against his stomach. He nodded back at de Groot, once, mouth set in a straight line. He looked annoyed. Jack wondered if it was because he could not fit through the front door.

'Nice place,' said de Groot, not even trying to sound like he meant it.

'Thanks. Nice bodyguard.'

'We have some business to complete.'

'Is that a question or statement?'

'I'm sorry I didn't get here on Saturday. Had to rush off for the weekend. Palm Beach.'

'I hate it when that happens.' Jack glanced at the goon outside the front door. He still had not moved.

'So,' said de Groot. 'Shall we do this?'

'Come into my office.' Jack gestured towards the counter.

Richard de Groot reached into his pocket: smug all over his tanned, clean-shaven face. He tossed a small wad of notes onto the counter, folded and held tight by a thin rubber band. 'Better not leave it lying around.'

There was probably about five hundred dollars there, give or take. Jack looked at the money and then at de Groot. Then he looked down at the money again. Strangely, he was neither shocked nor surprised. As his eyes traced over the topmost note, the situation came into focus smoothly, with a dull, nauseating knowing.

'Do you want to count it?'

Jack remained silent and continued to stare at the money. He was thinking a lot of things, though now it was mainly about the suited blond muscle man outside his front door, imagining the man had a thick Scandinavian accent.

De Groot leaned forward slightly, looking up from under the peak of his cap. 'Hello? Anybody home?'

Jack turned to him. Said nothing.

'I wouldn't complain, Mr Susko. You're lucky I even bothered to show up.' He turned to leave. 'Enjoy your bonus.'

Jack reached out and grabbed de Groot by the arm. He swung him around roughly.

'Don't be stupid, Mr Susko.' De Groot looked down to where Jack had gripped him, as though there was a stain. 'I don't like being touched.'

'I think you'd better get your wallet out.'

'Really?' Richard de Groot grinned and shook his head.

There was a noise: it was Jack's fist landing in the middle of de Groot's face, a snap 'n' crackle right jab, clean as a gust of sea breeze. Right in the honker. Something had come over Jack and he liked it. Pity he knew that the feeling was not going to last.

Before it ended, he gave de Groot a left to go on with. The South African hit the floor.

The front door opened. Sven the Destroyer walked into Susko Books. Or maybe it was Thor, God of Thunder. Whatever. The air around him bristled with sparks.

De Groot was trying to stand up. 'Get the prick!'

The immaculately suited bodyguard still had his sunglasses on. He was calm, expressionless, and surprisingly quick. He got behind Jack in a blur, wrapped an extremely thick arm around his neck, and pulled.

Jack grabbed the bodyguard's arm with both hands and started to writhe around a little, attempting to wrestle it off: the effort only seemed to tighten the grip around his neck. Seconds later, oxygen stopped flowing into his lungs. Another second, the muscles in his body started to drown in some kind of acid and his face felt like it was trying to peel itself off his skull.

'Son of a bitch!' De Groot held a handkerchief to his bleeding nose. He watched Jack struggle and swore some more. He blinked away some tears. Then he hawked up a mouthful of blood and spat it onto the floor of Susko Books. 'Hold him.'

One to the guts. It hurt because Jack could not curl down over the punch.

'What did you think, Susko? That I'd give you twenty thousand dollars for nothing?' Another for luck.

Jack groaned. He wondered if the guy holding him had started reading a book.

'Now you don't even get this.' De Groot picked up the money on the counter and slipped it back into his pocket. He shook his head lightly, dabbed at his bloody nose and looked around Susko Books. 'Jesus. Twenty grand,' he said, almost astounded. 'For what? Being in the wrong place at the wrong time? As though it was *my* fault.' De Groot tried to breathe through his nostrils and winced. 'Fuck!'

He spat on the floor again.

Noises were coming out of Jack's throat he was not trying to make. Like a wet balloon going down. He hoped the wind did not suddenly change and permanently set the grimace on his face. It would only add another thing to Jack's list, which set out clearly in point form his new, glowing hatred of de Groot and his family and every one of its extended relations, connected either through blood, marriage or employment.

Richard de Groot flicked his hand. The bodyguard let go of Jack's neck. He collapsed to the floor. He gulped down the stale air of Susko Books like it was spring water in a glass full of ice.

'Let's go, Lewis.'

The two men left. Jack tried to yell some abuse but his voice came out as barely a squeak. He struggled to his feet. As he stumbled towards the door, logic and the laws of physical inferiority told him to stay down and keep perfectly still, breathe slowly and act dead and pretend it never happened, just in case it happened again any time soon. But adrenaline had a hold of him. He climbed up the steps and onto the street just as de Groot was getting in behind the wheel of an illegally parked white Maserati Quattroporte. Lewis sat in the back, sunglasses still on, mouth a hard line, face a promise of cold pain. When he saw Jack through the window he simply waved his index finger: *Don't.* Jack heard the engine kick over. Somebody in the passenger seat leaned across Richard de Groot's lap and looked at Jack. It was just a second, barely even that, but he saw her.

Larissa.

What the hell?

Jack had never really believed that it was a small world. As far as he was concerned, the world had always been huge. But as he stood on dirty old York Street and watched de Groot's Maserati tear into the corner, he suspected he was going to change his mind in the next couple of minutes.

It took about three and a half. And then Jack knew for sure: everything was connected. The earth was a grain of sand.

~9~

Two hours later, she called.

'Hello, Jack.'

'Miss Larissa Tate.' He said it slowly. 'I was just thinking about you.'

A slight hesitation. 'How have you been?'

'Better. You?'

'Great.'

'That's good.'

'How's the book business?'

'Same as me,' said Jack. 'Going down in a slow blaze of glory.'

No response.

'You should have come in with de Groot,' he continued.

'Had a look around. I'd have given you a discount on a nice book.'

'I didn't know it was you.'

'Up until which point?' The words came out a little hot and fiery. 'When you read the name on the sign?'

'Don't be like that.'

'Boss or boyfriend?'

'Give me a break.'

'You first.'

Silence again. Jack remembered her body, the feel of her skin. They had met at a rooftop party in a Potts Point apartment, back in February. It was not the kind of crowd Jack usually found himself with — young, successful and wealthy — but an old girlfriend had invited him along, not wanting to arrive alone. At the bar, Larissa had asked him for a cigarette. Long, light-brown hair, fringe a perfectly cut straight line, right across the eyes, all smoky and dark. She was petite but curvy, wore a strapless black dress and heels that drew nice lines up and down her toned legs. She paid for the taxi home. She was fun. Jack had never been a toy boy before and was considering a full-time position when she pulled the plug on him a month or two later.

'Look, I'm sorry,' she said. 'What else can I say?'

'From fashion PR to driving around with the hard boys. Your job to watch out for the parking-meter guys?'

'I told you. I didn't know it was you.'

Jack frowned. 'Okay. Fine. Just go and tell your boss that I want my money.'

'It's not that simple.'

'Come round this end and take a look up the pipe.'

'Think I've got a better view?' Her tone sharpened.

'Just tell Richard de Groot that I want my money,' repeated Jack. 'And coming around with his goon isn't going to stop me getting it.'

Larissa clicked her tongue, softly. 'How does de Groot owe you money?'

'Come on. That's enough now.'

'Enough of what?'

'You were in the car, Larissa.'

'They told me *you* owed *them*. I could believe that.'

'*Jesus.*'

She cleared her throat. 'So what happened at the gallery?'

'What?' Jack's bullshit radar started beeping a little louder. 'What do you know about it?'

'Not much,' she said. 'I heard Richard on the phone to somebody in his office. Something about three guys wearing masks. Come on, Jack ...' She put on a little huskiness. 'We had a good time, didn't we?'

Jack shook his head. The New Feminism, in all its glory: better a caress than a kick to the balls. 'Yeah, they were done over. Three boys with a gun emptied the safe.'

'Did you see what was taken?'

'No. Something covered with a cloth, about the size of a phone book.'

She thought about that. Jack waited. He was tuned to her voice, concentrating on every nuance. He had not heard it for a while and it was nice to hear it again.

'What did the thieves look like?'

'Like thieves,' said Jack. 'Only ridiculous.'

'How?'

'One wore a Lone Ranger mask. The other two were off

to Mardi Gras later.'

'Are you serious?'

'Would have been funny if I hadn't been there.'

'So how does de Groot owe you money?'

'One of the heist guys took my book. A rare collectable. Dicky didn't want to call the cops. He offered to compensate me for my loss.'

Larissa almost laughed. 'And you believed him?'

Jack gritted his teeth.

'How much did he offer?'

'Enough.'

'Oh, Jack.'

He did not want to feel the fool, but felt it. Jack could see Larissa in his mind's eye, shaking her pretty head in that way she did, the fringe flicking across her eyes.

'We need to talk,' she said.

'About what?'

Over the phone, Jack heard muffled voices in the background. Then Larissa said: 'Gotta go.'

'Wait —'

'Call you tomorrow.'

The line was dead. Jack listened for a little while longer and then put the phone down. His radar was still sweeping the pulsing dot of Larissa on his screen. He was already looking forward to her call tomorrow. Whatever happened next, at the very least it was going to be interesting. And with any luck, Jack might even find out what the hell was going on.

He went over to the reference section in Susko Books, still feeling light-headed. He picked up the *Concise Oxford English Dictionary*: tenth edition, without the thumb index.

He did not bother asking a specific question. He just kind of held it, and thought vaguely about the Meaning of Life.

He opened the book. Finger down. Page 455.

edible/ • **adj.** fit to be eaten. • **n.** (**edibles**) items of food.
DERIVATIVES **edibility** n.
ORIGIN C16: from late L. *edibilis*, from L. *edere* 'eat'.

~10~

MAYBE IT WAS TIME TO GIVE THE GAME AWAY. Pick out a few good books, some clothes, make a couple of mix tapes for the Toyota, and then grab Lois and hit the road, Jack. Broome was the furthest place he could think of, a healthy five thousand kilometres away, straight across the continent. It would put a nice piece of distance between him and all the overdue notices pinned to the corkboard in the kitchen. And give Jack plenty of time to work out his plans for the future. Selling second-hand books was hardly the dream job he had fantasised about as a kid. But what had been? Secret agent? Rock star? Living legend? It was hard to remember with Larissa Tate's face bobbing around in his head like a champagne cork in a stormwater drain.

Jack slipped a thin worm onto his hook and cast out the line: tried De Groot Galleries in Woollahra again. This time, the call picked up.

'Yes?'

'Hello, Rhonda. Glad to see a little break and enter hasn't stopped you opening for trade.'

'Who is this?'

'Jack Susko. We were tied up together the other night. You, me and Max. Remember?'

Silence.

'How's Richard?'

'Fine, thank you.'

'That's good. He's a lovely man.'

'I'm very busy right now, Mr Susko. What do you want?'

'Well, I'm thinking I want to call the cops, Rhonda,' said Jack, evenly, so that each word was clear.

'I thought you settled all that with my husband.'

'So did I. But it looks like he changed his mind. A bit rude, really.'

'I'm sorry you feel that way,' she replied, not sorry at all.

'*That way* isn't the half of it, Rhonda.'

She laughed. 'I'm an art dealer, Mr Susko. My husband deals with his own problems. So unless you're interested in something you saw at the gallery —'

'Oh yeah, I'm interested,' said Jack. 'In the same thing you are. Has your husband told you what was in the safe yet?'

No reply. Jack let it hang for a moment. Then he said: '*Don't call the cops, don't tell the wife; here, Jack, here's some money to keep your mouth shut.* All sounds a bit dodgy, doesn't it?' He was making it up as he went along. 'What do you think?'

'You didn't hesitate to agree, Mr Susko.'

'I'm just a poor boy, Mrs de Groot. And somebody stole my shoes while I was asleep.'

'What a shame.'

Jack massaged his neck. Rhonda de Groot was tough as a rusted wheel nut.

'Goodbye, Mr Susko.'

'How do you get along with Larissa Tate?'

'Excuse me?'

'She works for your husband, doesn't she?'

'And how do you know Ms Tate?'

'Old friend.'

'I can imagine.'

'I sense a tone. Don't like her, Rhonda?'

'And what of it, Mr Susko?'

'Not sure. Why don't you like her?'

'I think I've had enough of this stimulating conversation.'

'Do you think she knew what was in the safe?'

A pause. Rhonda de Groot held the line. 'Why would you think that?'

'I don't. But it sounds like you do.'

For the second time that day, the line went dead in Jack's ear. And now he knew nothing about what was going on *twice*.

All he did know for sure was that it had been over three-and-a-half days since his last, smooth, soothing taste of tobacco. A personal best. No patches, no gum, no relaxation CDs — though plenty of St Agnes, the patron saint of Australian cooking brandies and drinkers on a budget.

Considering all that had happened in those three-and-a-half days, he was doing pretty well.

Three-and-a-half days. If anybody deserved a cigarette, it was Jack Susko.

~11~

THE NECK SQUEEZE AND THE COUPLE TO THE GUTS ensured a restless night. In Jack's bedroom, Tuesday morning felt like all the air had been sucked out of it. He had dreamed of an intersection with no lights, no give-way or stop signs, no cops with white gloves directing traffic. It was peak hour and Jack was right in the middle of it all, perched high on a penny-farthing, going nowhere fast as the cars and trucks screamed by. The *Penguin Book of Dream Interpretation* would not be necessary.

He got up early: made coffee, fed Lois, and put some music on; Django Reinhardt, twitching and twanging and strumming his guitar, like a man missing something he could never find, but was condemned to look for every time he played. A gypsy genius, bung hand and all. Even penniless, talent could pull a man through. Unfortunately for Jack, getting into *situations* did not constitute a talent.

The morning was already steaming and offered no respite from the blaring sun. Jack walked to work, down Oxford Street and through Hyde Park, sluggish and sore. Halfway there, he was sweating like a drycleaner at the steam press during Business Shirt Week. The place needed a storm to break. It was coming, he could sense it, but nothing was crackling in the air just yet.

At the Queen Victoria Building he dodged the young, beaming volunteers hanging around the entrance, shoving pamphlets and petitions and clipboards into everybody's path, covering every known guilt trip for affluent westerners that a university student could think of. He crossed York Street between the shuddering buses and ran across to Susko Books, still dark and cool in its hole, waiting for him. His haven. Jack hoped his current financial crisis would not force him to give it up any time soon.

There were no messages on the shop phone. He wondered when Larissa was going to call.

The first sale of the day put Jack in a better mood: a large woman in her late forties came in with a list. She had short brown hair and blue-grey eyes in a round, pleasant face. It was very red and she smiled a lot. A sleeveless green blouse, loose over black leggings, and hiking sandals. Jack helped her look. In the end, there were only two of the titles she had written down, but she had happily succumbed to three other books she found on her way around the shelves.

'I'm absolutely terrible,' she said. 'I cannot resist books!'

'It's a gene. Got a lot of relatives, by any chance?'

The lady laughed. 'Well, no … but there's my book club. They'd love it in here. Such an … an *eclectic* collection.'

'Eclectic is my middle name.'

She blushed a little, smiled some more. 'No, really, it's a lovely little bookshop.'

'Thanks. Just send the book club round.'

'Oh, I will. Except for Brianna.' Her bright faced dimmed. 'I'm sorry to have to say it, but she's such a snob. Wouldn't touch a second-hand book with a wooden spoon. Worried she'd catch something.'

'Tell her all the books are hosed down and come with a medical certificate.'

'I will! That's exactly what I'll say to her.'

Jack tallied her selection at the counter: *The Atlas of Legendary Places* by James Harpur and Jennifer Westwood; *Amarant: the Flora and Fauna of Atlantis*, edited by Una Woodruff; a slightly water-damaged copy of Gustave Doré's *Fables of La Fontaine*; the third edition of *The Elements of Style* by William Strunk Jr and E.B. White; and finally, *Covariance, Covariant and Covariation: the Mathematical Lives of Theodore and Sarah Newmarket* by Hugo Schiff. All up, seventy-five dollars. Jack dropped it down to sixty-five. Look after the customer and they will look after you.

'That's so kind.'

'A pleasure,' said Jack. 'Would you like a bag?'

'No, no, I've got my own, thank you.' She pulled out a cream canvas library bag. 'I carry everything in this. Books, groceries, you name it. Never broken a handle.'

She paid in tens and fives. Outside, she bent down and waved through the glass of the front door. Jack waved back. He felt like celebrating with a cigarette. He put a pencil to his lips and blew some imaginary smoke. Sixty-five smackers. The hourly rate worked out to twenty-one dollars and sixty-seven cents. A few more sales like that and Jack might soon be over the poverty line and mixing it big with the working class.

The day dwindled rather than grew. By the time the postman came by around 2.30 p.m. and slipped some mail under the door, the hourly rate was down to eleven eighty-two. About the same as collecting aluminium cans.

The mail consisted almost exclusively of bills. Bottom of the pile, a postal slip for the pick-up of a package. *Sorry we missed you. Available after 4.30 p.m.* Regular parcel, no signature necessary. Jack shook his head, slipped the card into his bag. How the hell had they missed him when he was there?

The rest of the day shuffled along to the late afternoon like an old man on a Zimmer frame. At 4.30 p.m. Jack was just thinking about shutting up early and heading for the post office when a couple of customers walked in. Maybe the day would end on the up after all.

Two men. One was tall and well-built; the other one was short and wide and round. The tall guy said: 'Hello, Jack.'

The tone was all wrong for a big-spending customer. 'Do I know you?'

'Not yet.'

Behind him, the fat guy had paused at the front door. He grabbed the handle and flicked the lock and then gave the handle a shake.

'What the fuck d'you think you're doing?' Jack moved

out from behind the counter.

'Where you were,' said the tall guy, who had flinty, deep-set eyes. He was wearing faded green, army-style pants and boots that looked like they could dent footpaths. He lifted the hem of his black, short-sleeved shirt. Jack saw a gun wedged into his belt and stopped.

'Who are you?'

'We're the cleaners.' The tall man stepped over to the discount table and swept his arm across it. Cheap paperbacks hit the floor like a small burst of dull applause. Then he kicked the table over. 'We're here to clean up.'

'What, the till? In a second-hand bookshop?' Jack frowned. 'This your first time?'

The man went over to a shelf and pulled more books off, one by one, and tossed them over his shoulder.

'Yeah, all right, I get the picture,' said Jack, raising his voice. Annoyance continued to outweigh his fear. 'It's behind the counter, all ninety-seven dollars of it. And you don't even need a key for the cash drawer.'

The guy kept throwing books to the ground.

'Jesus.'

Fat Boy came over, sweating profusely in a blue T-shirt the size of a small parachute. He wore red knee-length shorts and chunky white sneakers that looked like orthopaedic shoes for some kind of foot deformity. His calves were big and hairless and white.

His taller partner nodded without looking at him. The fat guy sighed, slumped his shoulders and walked over to the counter, moved in behind it and looked around. He crouched down with a groan and started searching through the shelves underneath.

'Is there anything I can help you with?'

The man stopped lobbing books over his shoulder. 'Where's the package?' he said. He leaned back against the now empty shelf, crossed his muscled arms and stared hard at Jack.

'What package?'

The guy grinned, then stretched out his arm and tapped his bare wrist. 'Five seconds.'

'I'm going to need a little more information.'

'Four seconds.'

Jack shook his head. *Fuck.* Then he remembered who the two guys were. 'Pascal and Walter,' he said. 'The dynamic duo. What happened to the masks?'

Pascal scratched his stubble. If he was surprised that Jack had recognised him, he did not show it. 'Three seconds.'

'How's Shane?'

'Two seconds.'

'There's nothing here,' said Walter from behind the counter.

'Time's up, Jack. The package or the fist?'

'I don't know what you're talking about.'

Walter stood up. 'It's not here,' he repeated. 'Maybe it hasn't arrived yet?'

'Keep looking.'

'What package?' asked Jack again. He remembered the postal slip in his bag. Kept it to himself.

Pascal adjusted the gun under his shirt but did not take it out. 'I'd talk if I were you.'

'About what?'

There was the sound of glass smashing behind Jack. Walter had knocked a picture off the wall.

'That's brilliant,' said Jack. 'Thanks.'

'Sorry.'

'What are you fucking apologising for?' said Pascal, annoyed.

'It was an accident.'

'You're the fucking accident.'

Walter's puffy face reddened. He gave Pascal the finger.

Jack stepped over to the counter, looked down at the floor. 'Nice one.' The frame held an original drinks menu from 1952 that he had found at a market in Rozelle: Lindy's on Broadway. Back then, an El Presidente cocktail set you back sixty cents. Scotch on the rocks, sixty-five. A pony of Rémy Martin VSOP, only seventy-five cents. Sometimes in his dreams, Jack went there and opened Susko Books right next door.

'Okay, so what now? You've smashed my place up and I don't know what the hell you're talking about.'

Pascal nodded at his colleague. 'Nothing there?'

'No.'

'All right, let's go, Walter. Mr Susko can explain himself personally.'

The Krauts knew how to build cars. Jack sat in the back of a sleek, dark-bronze Mercedes Benz CLS 500, in a climate-controlled, smooth leather cocoon with enough airbag crash technology to survive a collision with a small planet. The engine barely murmured. The suspension soaked up the aches and pains of the world like a warm sponge. It was the kind of car you could drive around in forever: and driving around forever did not seem like a bad idea to Jack right now.

They were heading down Botany Road, past warehouses and car dealerships and a few old redbrick pubs with satellite dishes on the roof but nobody inside. The traffic was thick with trucks and cabs and buses: their progress was slow. The only thing Jack could think of down this way was the airport.

'I only fly first class,' he said. His voice was light, but his stomach was tightly knotted. 'Did you grab my passport?'

No reply.

'Anybody got a cigarette?'

Pascal was in the back beside Jack. He turned his head a fraction. 'No.'

'Music?'

'There's only jazz,' said Walter, driving. 'I can't stand fucking jazz.'

They turned off Botany Road, took some lefts and rights down a couple of narrow streets and then came out onto another busy road, lined with construction work and airport hotels and furniture emporiums. Traffic was all first gear. Jack could see how hot it was outside — saw it in the long, tired faces of the cabbies, the sweat-slicked hair of the couriers in their shit-box vans and four-tonne trucks, the council workers in fluoro vests and shorts, dragging tattooed forearms across their brows as they paused digging a trench. For a moment, Jack was envious: it was honest work. You did it and then you were tired and then you slept. And then you did it again. But Jack also knew he could never be one of the guys he saw through the window. Outside, he would be leaning on his shovel, bored, wondering who was in the Mercedes with the tinted windows: how did they get there and what did they do and where were they going?

So. Now he knew.

Walter flicked the indicator on and nudged into the next lane. 'I'm going down King.'

'Do it.'

Full lock on the wheel, the Mercedes came to ferocious life and lunged forward in a tight turn, tyres smoking up the rear window. Jack leaned into Pascal as the car spun around, then straightened up as it took off down the street like a scalded cat.

Ten minutes later they stopped in front of a grey, aluminium-clad warehouse. A rusty mesh gate was closed across the driveway. Walter stepped out of the car and swung the gate open. He got back in and they drove through, over weedy gravel and blown-about rubbish, into the shaded cool of a large, concrete-floored loading area inside the warehouse. They stopped near a set of narrow metal stairs that climbed up the right-hand-side wall of the dock.

'Out you get, Jack.'

There was a white van parked beside an elevated loading ramp, but nobody around. A few crates here and there, hand-trolleys, a small electric forklift with its prongs half up, and a wire-fenced area in the far corner, filled with metal drums. The air was warm, smelt of grease and petrol, and seemed to thrum.

Walter started up the stairs, his feet clanging on the metal, the sound hollow and ominous. Pascal nudged Jack to follow. Halfway up, Jack wondered if he would bust anything if he jumped over the railing. He looked down and confirmed that he would. He started thinking about a plan B.

They reached the top of the stairs, walked along a narrow landing, and then Walter knocked on a door. 'It's us,' he said, up close, holding the handle like a gun pressed into somebody's back.

Jack heard a grunt. Walter opened the door. It was a large office space, with olive-green carpet and plasterboard walls and no windows. Two naked fluorescent tubes in the ceiling, over not much furniture. It could have used a pot-plant or two. But when Jack saw Shane Ferguson, he knew that nothing was going to help the bleakness in that room.

The bad actor was slumped in a chair. His nose was bloody and his shirt was torn. One of his eyes was a little swollen. Serious allergic reaction to something in the shape of a fist.

'Mr Susko. Welcome. My name is Viktor Kablunak.'

Jack turned to the voice. Behind a desk there was a man, shirt and tie and dark hair, leaning on his elbows. Eating a piece of barbecue chicken.

~12~

IT WAS A LONG, PLAIN, WOOD-LAMINATED DESK, the kind government departments auctioned off when they moved to newer premises. Viktor Kablunak sat behind it and worked his chicken. Drumstick and thigh. He ate like a man who had just returned from the Battle of Stalingrad. His small brown eyes were locked on Jack, but there was nothing to read in them. Blue-and-purple paisley tie over a white shirt. His shirtsleeves were rolled up past his elbows and his elbows were resting on the desk. Jack's copy of *From Russia with Love* was there, too. He hoped Kablunak had not been reading it while he ate.

'Nothing,' announced Pascal. 'We haven't checked his apartment yet, but I don't reckon it's arrived.' He glanced over at Shane tied up in the chair. 'Dickhead could only have sent it late on Friday or sometime Saturday, maybe Monday. So …'

Kablunak nodded, kept eating. There was a signet ring on the little finger of his right hand, a shield with the letters V and K inscribed, and a ruby set between them. Matching cufflinks were on the desk by his elbow. His hair was thick and healthy, dark with barely any grey, swept back over a square, Slavic skull. Large fleshy nose, cheeks a little flushed, jowls shaved and shiny. Fifty, or slightly older, but blessed with smooth-skin genes.

He kept eating the chicken. The rest of the carcass was splayed out in front of him on the desk, on a foil bag torn open down the middle. It was missing a couple of limbs and a good deal of breast. No vegetables or salad. Just the bird meat.

'Susko says he doesn't know anything about it,' said Walter.

Viktor Kablunak frowned and tossed what was left of the drumstick-and-thigh piece onto the desk, as though he had suddenly decided it was no good. He held his hands up, palms in like a surgeon about to go into theatre. He stared at Jack. Then he motioned for Walter to come over. Fat Boy leaned in behind the boss and reached into the breast pocket of his jacket hanging on the chair. He passed Kablunak a crisp white handkerchief and stood back. The boss snapped it open and wiped his mouth and his fingers and then blew his nose into it. He screwed up the handkerchief and dropped it onto the foil bag beside the chicken and began to roll down his sleeves.

'Vodka,' he said.

Walter went to a three-drawer filing cabinet in the corner. He slid open a drawer and got out a thick, stubby glass and a half-full, clear glass bottle. Stolichnaya. He poured Kablunak a drink. It went down in one gulp.

Jack swallowed a little of the heavy air in the room. 'Good read?' he said, pointing at his book on the desk.

Kablunak said nothing. He held out his glass for another shot. Walter poured. His boss emptied the glass again, smoothly.

'Mr Fleming,' said Kablunak. 'Yes. It is poor literature. But he knows what a man really is. Inside.' He spoke slowly and his voice was slightly accented, a touch stiff. Maybe English learned as a teenager, or studied in a foreign school. Either way, Viktor Kablunak sounded like a man who was used to being listened to. 'Inside,' he continued, tapping a thick thumb to his chest, 'man cannot forget completely that he is an animal that must fight to survive. Everything else is nothing.' He showed some good teeth. 'And James Bond … well. He knows that life has no consequence but death.'

Not quite the book report Jack was expecting. He stared at Kablunak as *no consequence but death* repeated in his head. 'You don't think that's a touch over the top?'

Kablunak ignored the question. He adjusted his cuffs, put the cufflinks in, clipped them, tugged at the sleeves of his shirt. He leaned back in the chair, wrists down on the edge of the desk, and sucked his teeth. Then he reached out and pushed the chicken a little further away. 'Did you know, Mr Susko, that Ian Fleming sold forty million books *before* Sean Connery made a fool of his creation in *Dr No*?'

'I knew he'd done okay.'

'That is much better than okay.'

'So you're a fan, then?'

'Well … I enjoyed your book.' He patted the copy of *From Russia with Love* on the desk.

'Good,' said Jack, trying not to think about the chicken grease on Kablunak's fingers. 'That'll be fifteen thousand dollars. Cash, if you can manage it.'

Kablunak smiled. 'No.'

Thoughts flapped around in Jack's brain like moths head-butting a light bulb. None of them held still long enough to let him formulate an idea. He turned and looked at Shane Ferguson again. Saw the swollen eye and the fat lip and the bloody dribble in the corner of his mouth.

'What happened to Shane?'

'Ah,' said Kablunak. 'You do know each other.'

'Not really,' said Jack.

The Russian nodded at Pascal. As Jack scanned Shane's face some more, a terrific punch filled his empty stomach and doubled him over. *Christ.* Hitting Jack in the guts seemed to be the latest craze. He tried to remain on his feet and wrapped his arms around his stomach, but the pain was there to stay and drew him kneeling to the floor. Kneeling did not help. Jack groaned and squeezed tighter as the hot pain grew. Hugging yourself was never the soothing experience you hoped it would be. For a couple of seconds he wondered if lying down and curling up into a ball might help, but remembered the head-stomping boots worn by Pascal.

'You have something of mine, Mr Susko,' said Kablunak. 'Something that was stolen from me. And now stolen again. I wish it returned.'

Pascal grabbed Jack hard by the bicep and pulled him to

his feet. Jack grimaced, his insides burning and a taste like battery acid in the back of his throat.

'Sorry, Jack,' said Shane Ferguson.

Kablunak put his hands behind his head and leaned back in the chair. He glanced down at the Fleming book on the desk and then reached over and smoothed the palm of his hand across the cover. 'Maybe you wish you were James Bond right now?' he said, voice light, but arrogant. 'Mr Susko?'

'We could pretend,' replied Jack, hunched over, wheezing. 'I'll be Bond,' he gasped. 'And you can be General … Grubozaboyschikov …'

Kablunak's brow tightened. He turned away, as though he was about to spit on the carpet. He took his time replying. 'If I was Grubozaboyschikov,' he said, evenly, 'you would be hanging on a hook right now.' He snapped a finger at the foil bag curled up around the chicken carcass.

Walter laughed. Kablunak gave him a look like a slap across the face. 'You think I'm funny?' he said. 'Grubozaboyschikov wiped out my father's village. With a pencil on the map.' Viktor Kablunak banged a fist down and slid his thumb across the desktop. 'Just like that. In one stroke. We had to run, like fucking animals. Those who stayed behind, the Chinese made dim sims out of their balls. But what would you know?' He shook his head, face dark with contempt. 'Here, history is all English lies.'

Silence. Jack tried to breathe quietly but the wheeze in his throat would not go away. He made a mental note to Google *Grubozaboyschikov* when he got home. Fleming obviously did a little research in between the martinis.

'Move this!' Kablunak waved his hand at the chicken.

Walter stepped over and quickly swept it up and dumped it into a small bin in the corner. The Russian glared down at the wood-veneer desktop. 'Where is my property, Mr Susko?'

The room was hot; Jack was sweating. 'I don't know what you're talking about.'

'Your friend here, Mr Ferguson, sent you something after he stole it from me. He is a very stupid man.' Kablunak paused, sighed. 'I hope *you* are not a very stupid man.'

The furniture in Jack's guts was all over the place, but they still told him not to mention the postal slip he got in the mail that day. 'Nobody sent me anything.'

'Don't lie to me, Mr Susko. Your friend lied. Did you look at him?'

Jack closed his eyes for a couple of seconds: Kablunak was still there when he opened them again. 'Yeah,' he said. 'I looked.'

'Good. Then no more bullshit, please.'

Jack remembered Richard de Groot not calling the cops back at the gallery; his wife not knowing what was in the safe. He remembered Pascal lifting a corner of the velvet cover on whatever the thing was and looking at it and smiling.

Jack turned to Shane. 'What the hell did you send me?'

'I'm sorry ... Jack ... I had no choice.'

'Does it hurt to talk?'

'Yeah.'

'Good. You owe me five hundred bucks from ten years ago. Why didn't you send me that instead?'

Shane coughed, swallowed with a little difficulty. 'I couldn't believe it was you at the gallery. Just give the package back to Mr Kablunak and everything will be sweet.'

'I haven't got any damn package!' Jack's anger focused on the beaten-up wannabe actor tied to the chair in front of him. 'What the fuck did you send me?'

Kablunak stood up, moved out from behind the desk and sat on the edge, one leg off the floor. 'You should not worry about details, Mr Susko. For you it is very simple. For now I will believe that you do not have what has been sent to you. So. When it arrives, you will call me. When I have it, you can forget about everything and go back to your life. Okay?'

'Sure, sounds great. But what if I don't believe you?'

'This is your problem.'

Jack stretched a little, ignited another spark of pain in his guts. How many problems was that now? Maybe he could get into the *Guinness Book of Records*. He nodded at the Fleming hardback on the desk. 'I'd like my book back.'

Kablunak half turned towards it. 'Yes, good,' he said, voice bright now. 'All I ask is a little cooperation. And then we can maybe have a fair exchange.'

'How about you give it to me now and *then* I cooperate.'

'No.'

'Okay,' said Jack, annoyed. 'In the meantime just promise to keep your greasy mitts off it.'

Kablunak raised an eyebrow, said nothing. Jack held his stare.

'Just do it, Jack.' Shane moved against the tape binding him to the chair. It rustled like aluminium foil.

Jack turned towards his former lodger. 'What's going on, Shane? I thought you wanted to be an actor.'

'I am an actor.'

'Obviously.'

Shane squinted up at Jack through his puffy eye. 'I needed cash. You know how it is.'

'So you got in on a heist and then tried to doublecross these guys?' Jack frowned in disbelief. 'Did you think you were in a movie?'

'Enough. Pascal and Walter will drive you home, Mr Susko.'

Jack looked at Viktor Kablunak. The Russian was inspecting his fingertips. He had broad, workers' hands, but manicured nails.

'What are you going to do with Shane?'

Kablunak grinned. Then stopped. He took his jacket off the chair behind the desk, reached into the inside pocket and handed Jack a card. 'Call this number when my package arrives. Do not open it, do not wait, do not *think*. Just call.'

Pascal leaned into Jack's face. 'Reckon you can handle that?'

'Yeah. No problem. Reckon you could brush your teeth?'

This time, even Viktor Kablunak grimaced at the punch.

~*13*~

THEY DROPPED HIM OFF IN THE CITY. It was going-home time. Ties loose, jackets off, faces relaxed. High heels swapped for sneakers. Tourists stared at the menus taped to restaurant windows, deciding where to eat. A million text messages beeped on a million phones as the city's population stared down into the palms of their hands. Jack wondered if a Russian gangster had threatened anybody else today.

He waited for a bus: when it came, he slumped into a seat and stared out the window as it crawled up Oxford Street through the peak-hour traffic. By the time he got to Paddington the sun was fading, its pale tawny light thickening across the sky. Jack stumbled home under the muted glow, washed out and a little fragile, like a paper serviette left in a pocket and gone through a rinse cycle.

He pulled out his keys and was about to unlock the front door of his apartment in Leinster Street, when he noticed a thin stripe of weak light running the length of the jamb. He pressed his fingertips to the door, applied the barest pressure: the hinges creaked. All of Jack's senses woke simultaneously. His skin prickled and his ears popped and all his muscles pulled tight against his joints. Forgetting to lock up was just something Jack never did. Not sober, anyway. He listened, then pushed the door and waited at the threshold as the slow arc of its opening revealed what was going on inside.

He looked: none of it was good.

The front room was like below decks on a beached boat, everything slipped from the shelves and spilled across the floor. Jack swore and stepped carefully between the books and albums and furniture lying silent and vulnerable, as though passed out after a party. Kablunak's boys, earlier in the day?

No. He remembered them telling the Russian they had only searched Susko Books. Somebody else had been here. And no doubt for the same reason. Mysterious-package hunting.

He walked over and opened the sliding door to his small, paved rear yard and let a whining Lois into the flat. She miaowed, shook herself and then stretched from the tip of her nose to the splayed claws of her extended hind legs, each in turn. After a quick lick at something bothering her front paw, she pit-patted straight into the kitchen and sniffed at her food bowl, paying no attention to the rearrangement of the décor. She sat down and miaowed again, pots and pans and broken cups strewn around her. She looked up at Jack, let him read her face: *It wasn't me.*

Jack lifted the flap of his bag and pulled out the postal slip. Inspected it. No clues there, but considering the interest level, it was probably better to leave whatever it was at the post office for the time being. Kablunak could wait. Jack had a strong feeling that the mysterious package might be the only chip he had to throw down if push came to any more shove. He slipped it back into his bag.

He went into the kitchen: tinned seafood platter for Lois and an egg-and-mayonnaise sandwich on toasted stale bread for himself. Then he started to clear up the mess. He carefully stacked his albums, first inspecting each record. He picked up *This Is Sinatra*, 1953, half under the couch and slipped out of its sleeve. A bit of dust, but no serious damage. He had not heard it in a while. The turntable was on top of the sideboard and had escaped the intruder's attention. Jack put the record on and turned up the volume. He listened to the warm scratch and crackle of the needle biting into the vinyl and then settling into a hairy groove that popped the speakers lightly. It was making him feel better already. The sound of delicious tension. Then the big brass kicking in. And then softly, softly, everything down low — and Frank, with all that tone.

Got the string around my finger …

More like a noose around his neck. Jack thought about cigarettes again, felt a knot of wanting tighten his broken guts, and then tried to forget about it as he continued clearing up.

There was a knock on the door a little while later. Jack turned the volume down on the stereo. He found Larissa Tate standing in the hall.

'Hello there,' said Jack. He managed to keep his tone neutral, but his heart gave a couple of thumps in his chest. 'Come in.'

She reached over and put a hand on his arm. A little squeeze, leaned in, a peck on the cheek. Jack reciprocated. He could feel the coolness of the hallway on his face.

'You look good, Jack.'

'I've been working out.'

No comment. She walked in.

Jack swept his eyes over her. 'Look good yourself.'

Her movements were relaxed. She was wearing a silk halter-neck top, the print some kind of equestrian number with buckles and saddles and riding helmets all over it. A pair of bleached-blue, tight 1980s-style jeans. On her feet, jade-green, flat peep-toe shoes. Same light-brown, long silky hair with the serious fringe. Same dark eyes and glossed lips, same easy, unconcerned expression on her face. And the same petite, toned body, though the curves were fuller. Sexier.

The nearly twelve months that had passed since they parted had been good to Larissa Tate.

Jack closed the front door. 'How's Richard? You should have brought him along.'

Larissa smiled: stretched lips only, small and brief. She tossed her handbag onto the couch. 'I've been trying your mobile, the shop, no answer ...'

'Late lunch. Making new friends.'

'Was she attractive?'

'I didn't like the way she ate her chicken.'

Larissa stood in the middle of the lounge room, her back to him. 'Didn't realise you were so fussy.'

'I've changed. It's all about *me* now.'

She turned side on, smiled at that one. 'Glad to hear it.'

Jack sat down in the Eames chair. 'Mr Muscles out in the car?' he asked.

'Why? Do I need a bodyguard?'

'Maybe the new me is a homicidal lunatic.'

'Uh-huh.'

She sat down on the two-seater couch. Leaned back, crossed her legs. She pointed her chin at Jack and flicked her hair.

'So. Would you like to know what was stolen out of the safe at De Groot Galleries?'

Larissa Tate was a piece of work. Jack liked her. A lot, and counting.

'What?' he said.

'A Bible.'

He let the news sink in. 'What kind of Bible?'

'A very expensive kind,' said Larissa. She smoothed a thigh with the palm of her hand. 'Gold boards, jewel-encrusted, illuminated, immaculate. A one-off masterpiece by a famous Russian monk. Thirteen ninety-six. It's called the Sergius Bible.'

'A hobby of yours?'

She shrugged.

'How much?

'About a hundred thousand dollars.' She tossed off the amount as though leaving a tip for the waiter.

Jack thought *Jesus*, but said: 'Is that all?' A bad feeling tightened the muscles in his neck. It was the kind of money people *did* things about. The kind of money to maybe get out of the way of.

'Well?' said Larissa.

'How do you know all this?'

'The internet is amazing.'

Jack frowned. A muscle twitched in his leg.

Larissa uncrossed hers, brought her knees together and leaned forward on her elbows. 'Look, last time we spoke —'

Jack held up his hand. 'Hang on. Answer me something. Why wouldn't de Groot insure a thing like that?'

She took a long breath, exhaled. 'Because it's stolen.'

The words seemed to have an echo to them in Jack's ears. He listened until they faded.

'That's what I wanted to talk to you about,' said Larissa.

'De Groot deals in stolen art?'

'Yes.'

'Here?'

Larissa straightened up. 'Don't be naïve, Jack.'

Jack thought of Viktor Kablunak. A small ball of fire glowed in his stomach. 'Naïve would be nice.'

'Hundred thousand,' repeated Larissa. 'A hundred and twenty-two, as matter of fact. Last time I checked the exchange rate.'

Jack watched her face. She did not seem overly concerned about anything. The room was hot but it was all cool façade over on the couch with Larissa.

'One and a bit, huh? Just like that. You know all about it and you couldn't wait to come around and tell me.'

'We're old friends, aren't we, Jack?' She grinned, looked him over.

'How long have you been working for de Groot?'

'Long enough.'

'Long enough that he'd tell you all about his art-smuggling business?'

Larissa Tate rolled her eyes.

'You know, but the wife doesn't?'

'Rhonda?' she scoffed. 'I'm an employee of De Groot Finance. Not a marriage counsellor.'

Jack kept his mouth shut, but his face must have whispered something.

'Don't even think it,' said Larissa, raising her voice again. 'I don't have to fuck anybody I don't want to.'

'That doesn't mean you haven't.'

'No. It doesn't.' Larissa scratched the palm of her hand. 'Have you spoken to Rhonda?'

'We're in counselling together,' said Jack. 'After the trauma of the heist.'

'It would pay to be straight with me.'

Outside, the day waned and headed for the horizon, its heat dragging behind like a heavy cloak. Jack's apartment felt oppressive.

'You start,' he said. 'All I see is curves.'

'You don't like them?'

'I'm the nervous type.'

'Not how I remember it.'

'So now it's okay to flash it about, huh? A moment ago I offended you.'

'You assumed. But now you know.'

Jack shook his head. 'What do you want, Larissa?'

She looked down into her lap. Then she flicked her hair and sat up straighter. 'Money,' she said.

'Ah. The ol' five-letter word.'

'We need to do a deal, Jack.'

He nodded. At least she did not want to punch him in the stomach.

'De Groot makes *shit*-loads of money. Religious art is his speciality. Eastern Europe is being completely ransacked and collectors are flush, willing to pay big dollars. And everybody wants to go to town on the Sergius. They're lining up for it.'

'I thought you used to work for a fashion magazine.'

'I've got an honours degree in economics.'

'Majoring in …?'

'International banking and being my own woman.'

'Right. And now you're specialising in stolen art?'

'Just this once.'

'Meaning?'

Larissa stood up. 'I've diverted a little piece off the de Groot stolen-art conveyor belt.'

'Diverted?'

She looked around. 'Have you got something to drink?'

Jack pointed to the dining table. His bottle of St Agnes was there.

Larissa got up, walked over and looked at the bottle. 'My grandmother used to put this stuff in her puddings.'

Jack shrugged. 'So you know it won't kill you.'

'You're all class.' Larissa unscrewed the cap and splashed brandy into a couple of glasses. 'But listen to me, Jack, and you'll be buying the good stuff.' She walked over and handed him a drink. She remained standing beside the Eames chair.

'Cheers.'

She clinked her glass against his. 'So. Usual stuff with the stealing and dealing,' she said. 'Just another day at the office. But Richard didn't do the Sergius just for money. He wanted to send a message.' Larissa drank some brandy. 'An old rival is on the scene and he's getting rich very quickly. Too quickly. And Richard's losing clients.'

Jack grinned. A couple of jigsaw pieces had come together. 'The Sergius was stolen from another art thief?'

'Yep. Which means nobody is going to involve the law, Jack. You understand? It's like an apple from the neighbour's tree just fell into your yard.'

'Doesn't mean he won't come around to get it back.'

'I'll be gone by then.'

Jack sipped his brandy. 'This other art thief,' he said. 'Guy named Viktor Kablunak, by any chance?'

It took her by surprise. She still looked good. 'You know him?'

'My new best friend.'

'Shit.'

Jack drank a little more. 'And what about Shane Ferguson?'

She frowned.

'That's what I thought. Just so you know, he's tied up in a chair at Kablunak's warehouse. He didn't look too good. Pretty sure he wasn't feeling any good, either.'

Larissa's face paled.

'Which means Kablunak knows all about the …' Jack pretended not to remember. 'What's it called again?'

'The Sergius.'

'Yeah. The Sergius. And how Shane sent it to me.'

She chewed her bottom lip. 'Have you got it?'

'No. Still on its way.'

A pause. The thoughts sparking her brain worked to brighten her grim face. 'So we can still do this, Jack!'

'We?'

~14~

LOIS CAME OUT OF THE BEDROOM, vague, eyes half-open. She stopped and yawned. Licked herself. She walked over and nudged Larissa's shins and then plopped down onto a cushion on the floor.

'Still got the fleabag, then.'

'Lois is a recovering alcoholic. I'm helping her get back on her paws.'

'I'll give you twenty thousand dollars.'

'Not my lucky number, lately.'

'Fine. Twenty-one thousand. That'd buy a few first editions, Jack. Or you could spruce up the bookshop. Or maybe take a holiday in Positano. I'm sure you deserve one.'

Jack smiled, rubbed his chin. 'Still leaves you a clean

hundred thousand, though, doesn't it? Sure twenty-one grand is fair?'

'You don't think twenty-one thousand dollars is enough for doing absolutely nothing?'

'Is that what you want me to do?' Jack stood up, went to the brandy bottle on the dining table and poured himself some more. 'I want fifty.'

'You think this is a joke?'

'No. I think I'm the cheese in everyone's toasted sandwich.'

'So why don't you give me a bite?'

Jack looked at her. She had moved from one-off payment to partnership in the flick of a fringe. 'Come on, Larissa. Now who's being silly?' But the idea still floated on his stock exchange. Just as she knew it would.

'Why not?' She looked around. 'I don't see any girlfriends anywhere.'

Jack drank, watched Larissa over the glass. She was doing that dark, smoky, sexy eyes thing again, with just a splash of woe-is-me. He put the glass down on the dining table. 'You got cigarettes?'

'No.'

'So you know Shane Ferguson, huh?'

A pause. She looked disappointed. 'Yes, from acting. We're members of the same company in Surry Hills. The Palomino Theatre.'

'You act?'

'Don't look so shocked. I'm actually pretty good.'

'I don't doubt it.'

'We did *The Merchant of Venice* last season. I was Portia. Got a small write-up in the paper.'

'Any masked-ball scenes?'

'What?'

'Nothing. Congratulations. Now tell me why Shane Ferguson would send me a stolen Bible in the mail?'

Larissa sighed, heavily. 'Because they were on to him at the last minute.'

'What happened?'

'After the job, Shane was going to grab the Sergius and take off for his shoot in China. Sit on it until I got there. I'd given him a package that looked like the original and he stashed it at the warehouse. Quick one two, done.'

'That must have taken months of planning.'

'Look, it was simple and perfect and everything was covered, trust me. The guys he was working with were *casual*. Anyway, I don't know what happened exactly, but they were on to him at some point and followed his cab to the airport. Luckily Shane noticed the car. He gave the driver a bunch of fifties and asked if he could send a package for him. Obviously not to his home or mine. He'd remembered you from the night of the job and some book they took off you. The address of your shop was in it.'

'*From Russia with Love.*'

'That's the one. He called me on the mobile and let me know. I assumed he'd just gone to China.'

'And here you are.' Jack looked around his flat. Larissa had set it all up sweet: for herself. 'How did Shane get involved with the guys doing over de Groot?'

'He knows one of them, and they swung him on board.' Larissa scratched an eyebrow with her little finger.

'Why'd he do it? You talk him into it?'

'*Moi?*'

'Yeah, Ms *Moi*.'

'Fifteen years of trying to be an actor has got him into serious debt. He's thirty-five, broke, and not very talented. He wanted the quick fix. Nothing to do with me.'

'And what about you?'

Larissa shrugged. 'No more working for the man, Jack.'

'You would have trusted Shane with the Sergius?'

'What was he going to do with a priceless stolen Bible? Put it on eBay?'

Jack poured more brandy. He held up the bottle for Larissa. She came over with her glass. She stood closer to him than was necessary.

'So Shane was your ticket.'

'He was my *in*.'

'And you were going to take care of the rest?'

'That's right. Everything hooked up nicely.'

'Except now I've got the Sergius.'

Larissa nodded. She bent one of her legs so that the knee brushed him. She kept her eyes on his face.

Jack gazed over the smoothness of her neck, the milk-and-honey skin, the softness of her full lips. 'I've already told you,' he said. 'It's not here.'

'We could wait for it together?'

'It's only a one-bedroom flat. And Lois has got the couch.'

'So what's the problem?'

She tilted her head back. They kissed. Slowly. Longingly. It was a nice change from Jack's recent work as a human punching bag. They kept kissing. They got better at it. Jack was full of mixed emotions: but for now, at least his lips knew what the hell was going on.

~15~

WEDNESDAY MORNING. Instead of Larissa, there was an old book beside Jack. And a note: *I'll call later. Thought you might like a couple of interesting facts!* Jack picked up the book: *The New Banbury Dictionary of Saints and Sinners*, edited by Stefan Williams. He sat up a little in bed. Second edition, 1975, Banbury Cross Press, Illinois, USA. Fifteen dollars, written in pencil on the title page. No dust jacket, just the threadbare, cloth-bound boards, faded to pale ochre red, the corners frayed and a little squashed. Title and author stamped on the front and spine in dull gold lettering. Yellow-cream end papers, and glued onto the rear inside sleeve, an old yellow library loan pocket — catalogue number 823.89, R746h, Pepperdine University Library, Malibu, California 90265.

*Note to borrowers: overdue rate: 25c per day. Total fine cut 50%
if paid when book is returned.* A stamp indicated that at some
point the book had ended up at the Tecolote Bookshop,
De la Guerre Studios, Santa Barbara. And now momentarily
with Jack Susko, via Larissa Tate, Sydney, Australia. Even
inanimate objects got to see more of the world than Jack
did.

He flipped it open at the bookmark. Page 217.

Sergius the New, monk; b. 1322, Smolensk; d. 1396, Zargorsk;
cd. 1443; f.d. 15 January.

Named Boris at birth, Sergius the New suffered a childhood
of great poverty and hardship. The family was poor and moved
around frequently, often forced to flee surrounding villages due to
the father's mental illness and the horrible stigma attached to his
condition. The city authorities eventually arrested him and placed
the unfortunate sufferer in a sanatorium in 1329: to survive,
the mother was thus forced to give some of her eight children
away. Boris, the youngest, was left on the hard stone steps of the
Monastery of the Holy Ghost, where he soon entered the order.

Not long after, legend tells us, he was discovered in the
Scriptorium during a particularly cold winter's night, sleeping
by the fire. (The Scriptorium was the only room in the entire
monastery that was heated.) The subsequent punishment he
received, particularly brutal and reserved for only the most
heinous of sinners, was forty-two lashes with the branch of
a frozen birch tree. It is said that at the height of his pain and
delirium, God appeared to him: He instructed Sergius to
illuminate the Bible, '... with the light of the glory of He who sits
upon the throne of the world and is worthy.' [Theo. *Ecc. II. et. iv. 7*]
Sentenced to further punishment for mouthing such blasphemy,

Sergius was reprieved in the eleventh hour, after the abbot was visited by God in a dream and instructed to return Sergius to the Scriptorium and have him taught in the art of illumination. It is said the abbot was shown a vision of the Great Fires of God's Wrath. God's wish was thus duly executed.

Sergius the New became renowned as a young monk for the straightness of his lines, drawn freely and without technological aid, with either his left or right hand. Controversially, the manuscript paper was set on an angle across his scriptorium desk. (This eventually became standard procedure.) Other innovations included a cushion, made of hessian and filled with warm mulch and straw, that added nearly three hours to a monk's productivity; and inserts cut into the heavy oak of the scriptorium desks, for the secure placement of ink pots, which resulted in so significant a reduction in the rate of accidental spillage and manuscript damage that Sergius was called before the Bishop of Smolensk and praised before a gathering of abbots. This led to his appointment, in 1354, as Grand Scribe at the Trinity Monastery of Zargorsk, where he would spend the remainder of his life and also complete God's Work: culminating in his masterpiece, the illuminated Holy Book that has since become known as the Sergius Bible. It took forty-two years to complete and was finished on the very day of his death in 1396.

In 1621, Sergius the New was pronounced patron saint of arthritis sufferers. The Vatican investigated the Sergius Bible in 1967, after a succession of miracles were attributed to it by those who read its pages. It was pronounced a Holy Relic in 1974.

Jack closed the book, dropped it onto the bed beside him and slid back down under the sheet a little. *The Sergius Bible*. He thought about what it would feel like to hold. All one hundred and twenty-two thousand dollars' worth of it. All six-hundred-plus years' history of it. And he wondered — if he asked nicely — would Viktor Kablunak maybe lend it to him for the weekend?

~16~

THE WORLD WAS LIKE A GIANT FAN-FORCED OVEN. Thick, serious clouds had already started to pack the sky on the horizon, climbing up and up on top of one another, pressing the lower clouds into a shadowy grey. Humidity squeezing out of them, like wringing a sponge.

He sat down for breakfast at a café in the QVB, bustling with tourists. Bright and shiny, except for Jack. Checked the menu but only had the appetite for a long black and a croissant. He lingered with the paper, got into Susko Books late. Crossed York Street, glanced up at the clock on Town Hall: 10.40 a.m. As usual, there was no crowd waiting impatiently for him to open up.

But there was some fresh graffiti, on the wall beside

the steps leading down to Sydney's finest-quality book emporium. It said: *LET IT GO*. When Jack unlocked the front door and stepped inside, he wondered about his chances. As he looked around the place, he did not think they were very good.

Susko Books was all over the floor. Rifled. Ransacked. *Ravaged*. The anger swelled in Jack's chest like a heart attack. A few aisles had been spared, but the rest had been roughly cleared. The counter, too, was a mess of papers and invoices and bills, dumped out of the expanding files that were stored underneath. The drawers of the filing cabinet under the desk were pulled out and drooping off their runner-grooves like a couple of emptied pockets. Spilt wine always looked like more than had been in the glass, and Jack now knew the same was true of books. He gazed around, silent, a little amazed to see just how many books there were. As though he had never sold one in his whole life.

Viktor Kablunak? But his boys had already been around. And it was clear that Kablunak was going to injure Jack if he did not deliver the Sergius to him. So who? The same party that had broken into his apartment? Who else knew about the Sergius — and, more to the point, who else knew that Jack had been sent the thing? Shane Ferguson naturally did, but Jack seriously doubted this was any of his work. Then there was Larissa, but she had Jack as an alibi for the whole night gone. Maybe she had told somebody? Maybe Richard de Groot himself? Jack could visualise his bodyguard Lewis going to town on his bookshelves, looking for the Bible. But why would Larissa tell de Groot? She was attempting to steal the thing from him, after all …

He walked towards the counter, trying not to step on his stock. He bent down and picked a few books off the floor and carried them over. Put them down, gently. He noticed a slim, wrinkled, black-covered paperback that had seen better days. *Fragments* by Heraclitus. Maybe that was what Jack needed, at this difficult time. Ancient insight. A little universal wisdom. He flipped the book open and planted his finger. Page 6.

χρυσὸν γὰρ οι διζήμενοι γην πολλὴν ορύσσουσι καὶ ευρίσκουσιν ολίγον.

Never the straight answer.

After a while, Jack's anger settled a little. The adrenaline in his body began to clear. Then something occurred to him: how did they get in? He went over to the front door again and had a look. The lock was intact. He ran to the rear door that opened out onto Market Row, the more likely break-and-enter spot. Locked tight. What the fuck?

Somebody had got in with keys. Maybe the same keys that had been used on Leinster Street. Apart from the ones in Jack's pocket, there were only two other spare sets. One was back at the apartment, in the top drawer of the sideboard. The other set was in the glove box of the Toyota.

~17~

COUSIN CARL WAS AN ELECTRICIAN. He had a small advertisement in the *Yellow Pages*. Jack tried the mobile listed but the call rang out to the message bank. *Leave your name, number* … Carl did not sound as though he enjoyed being an electrician. Jack did not leave a message. He looked up *Reiss, C.* in the *White Pages* and found a residential number and address. He wrote down the address. No calls. Better if he went over personally. It was definitely more a man-to-man situation.

Carl's house was in Bankstown. Too far, too hot and too urgent for public transport. Jack needed wheels. He picked up the phone and called Ray Campbell.

'Still on the margaritas?'

'Why, of course, Jack. The good ship Campbell is passing pleasantly through the Panama Canal, and all on board are relaxed and happy.'

'So you don't need your car, then?'

'Not at this point in time, no. But you do?'

'Need to get somewhere.'

'It's overrated, Jack. And eventually, you always get back to where you began.'

'That's fine. I just don't want to spend too much time on the return trip.'

'Rush, rush. The modern affliction.'

'I need it for the afternoon. Any chance?'

'Every. Except that it's broken. Sorry, Jack.'

'You didn't crash the Daimler?'

'No, no, nothing like that. It's the electricals. I turned the headlights on the other night and the fan started up. Flicked the indicator and got the windscreen wipers. And then the starter motor caught fire.'

'The Brits have never understood electricity.'

'The main thing is that I'm all right.'

Jack was disappointed. The Daimler was a 1973 Sovereign 4.2 — a real motor, big and bronze, like driving around in a lounge room. The leather seats were cracked and the body was rusted and you did not get very far on a hundred bucks' worth of fuel, but even a bum could feel like a king behind the wheel. 'How much to repair?' he asked.

'I don't want to think about it whilst I'm on holidays.'

'Fair enough.' Jack moved some books around on the counter. 'Listen, Ray. You ever heard of the Sergius Bible?'

'Well, I should hope so. I'm not just a second-hand bookseller, you know.'

'There are plenty of things you're not, Raymond.'

'*Touché.*' But Ray heard something in his tone. 'Are you down in the dumps, son?'

Jack looked around Susko Books. 'Something like that. So what do you know, but minus the history lesson. I've read up on that.'

'The more current facts? It was stolen last year from the monastery of Zargorsk in beautiful Russia. And in broad daylight, mind you.' There was a shuffling noise down the line. 'Hang on. Let me get the magazine. I'm pretty sure it was in the latest *Time.*'

Jack waited a moment. He was in a hurry to get to his cousin's place, but was keen on any extra information about the Sergius. Not that he had any idea how it might help him.

Ray picked up the phone again. 'Here we are.'

'You read *Time* magazine?'

'I got a subscription for my birthday. It's the thought that counts.'

'What's it say?'

'A moment please, let me find it.' Ray hummed as he flipped through the pages. 'Let's see ... article on the decline in world oil production ... the decline of sperm rates in western males ... the decline in the nutritional value of fruit and vegetables ... the decline of the US, world financial markets, and the environment, too. Oh look, even Hollywood is going down the toilet.'

'Sounds like the world's gone to crap.'

'Whatever happened to the nice stories?' asked Ray. 'About alien abduction in small rural towns? And pandas that finally got off their arses and did their duty for the species?

And where are all the cartoon strips? Whatever happened to Andy Capp, lying around on the couch with his back to the world?'

'You retired from public life.'

'Very funny.'

'Come on, Ray. I'm in a hurry.'

'Here we are, here we are. Page 36. "The Not So Divine Comedy" by Dahlia Wallis. And I quote: *The international black market in religious art is doing a roaring trade. Thanks to poor security and unceasing demand from collectors, thieves are brazenly helping themselves to some of the oldest and most precious works in the world. Eastern European churches in particular are being targeted. And, it seems, there is not much out there to stop them: neither security nor shame. "There is no fear of the police anymore, it doesn't exist," says Father Constantine Gligoris. "The thieves fear nobody, not even God."'*

'Where's the bit about the Sergius?'

'Um ... here. There's a list of stolen work and its value. A Caravaggio nativity scene worth an estimated twenty million, stolen in Palermo. Two-point-seven million for a jewel-encrusted painting of the Virgin Mary and Baby Jesus, stolen from a cliff-side monastery in Montenegro. A priceless Last Supper. A one-point-nine-million-dollar Black Madonna. Various crosses and censers and woodcut Stations of the Cross. And, here it is, the Sergius Bible. One-point-seven million euros.'

Jack stopped breathing for a moment. 'Excuse me?'

'One-point-seven. That's nearly three-and-a-half million dollars, give or take.'

Silence.

'Actually, three-point-four, at the current exchange.'

Silence.

'Jack? Hello?'

'That's a lot of money.' Jack's voice was hoarse, as though he had smoked a whole packet of cigarettes in the last five seconds.

'I quote again ...' said Ray. '*It is all part of an illegal industry that was estimated to turn over somewhere in the realm of six billion US last year.*'

A small tidal wave passed through Jack's brain. He sat down. 'Some realm,' he said.

Ray continued: '*More often than not, armed gunmen simply walk in and then walk out. The OCBC, France's Central Office for the Fight against Traffic in Cultural Goods, believes that much of the demand is being driven by the new super-rich of Russia, who are said to pay handsomely to furnish their summer dachas with exclusive holy artefacts.*'

Jack could feel a clamp on his head, heard the squeak of screws as it tightened around his temples. 'I've got an old commemorative Communion picture,' he said. 'Angels blowing some golden trumpets. What do you think?'

Ray laughed. 'At least a hundred thousand.'

'That's what I thought.'

'So why the interest in Bibles?'

Jack licked his dry lips. 'A ... customer asked about the Sergius.' He struggled to make something up. 'Wanted to know if there were any books on it.'

'Do you want me to send the article to you?'

'No ... that's fine. Thanks, Ray.'

'Sorry about the car.'

'No problem. I've got one other option. Should be fine.'

'Drive carefully.'

'Always.'

Three-point-four million dollars. No wonder people were messing up his things. Was Jack the only one who had no idea?

He stepped out of the frame for a moment and looked. Yep, there he was. Piggy in the goddamn middle.

It was not a call Jack wanted to make. He knew Chester Sinclair well and asking the man for a favour was the equivalent of having to saw your own leg off. Shylock had nothing on this guy.

'Hello?'

'Chester. It's Jack.'

'Well, well. Mr Susko. What a pleasant surprise.' Already the voice was smug. Jack hardly ever called and Sinclair's antenna had immediately picked up that he probably needed something.

'How are things?' asked Jack.

'Tight, of course, tight. The current economic downturn is really putting the squeeze on, Jackie boy. Consumer spending, up the shit. Woe the Bookstalk, my friend, woe the Bookstalk.' He sighed. 'But we must keep our heads.'

'Mmmm,' said Jack, wishing again that he had never mentioned his idea for a bookshop name — Jack and the Bookstalk — in front of Sinclair, who had stolen it without remorse or regret. But that was just the kind of guy Chester Sinclair was. As he held the phone to his ear, Jack was still considering whether he should ask the man for a favour. He could almost see Sinclair's pasty, indoor complexion gain a touch of colour as Jack humbly begged for the loan of his car.

'What about you, Jack?' asked Sinclair. 'Up or down?'

'Floating in it.'

'Watch the tidal waves.'

'I've got a good plank of wood.'

'Hold on tight.'

Jack rubbed his face. 'Your car still go, Chester?'

'My car?'

Jack heard the antenna in Sinclair's head start to hum. 'I need to borrow it. Just for today. Three or four hours, max.'

'What for?'

'Need to pick something up.' Jack kept his voice neutral.

'I see.' Sinclair cleared his throat. 'Well, I was going to need it today. It would *definitely* put me out.'

'What do you need it for?' Jack indulged him. The haggle for price was inevitable and he wanted it over quickly.

'My mother needs to go to the doctor.' Sinclair had decided on the sympathy angle. 'She's quite ill.'

Ever since you were born, probably. Jack said: 'And you're such a good son.'

'Well, one must help where one can.'

'I'll fill it up on the way back.'

'Plus fifty.'

Jack shook his head. 'That's just greed, Sinclair. I could get a hire car for that. And it wouldn't be a piece of shit.'

'Yeah? So why don't you?'

Son of a bitch. Jack would have, except he had no room left on any of his three red-lining goddamned credit cards. He breathed his anger down. 'Because I'd rather fill a friend's tank,' he said. It was a poor effort at sincerity and everybody listening knew it.

Chester scoffed. 'Full tank plus fifty.'

'I don't want to *buy* your car, Sinclair.'

'Going ... going ...'

Jack glanced at the clock. Nearly 11.30 a.m. *Fuck*. He really did hate Chester Sinclair. 'Okay, okay. Done.'

'And I need you to drop something off for me on the way.'

'Don't push it, Sinclair.'

'Take you five minutes, that's all.' He paused for a moment. 'Drop the fifty off to Eddie.'

'Are you serious?'

'What? You're paying the fifty, it's my money, and I want to give it to Eddie.'

'Randwick isn't on my way.'

'Yeah, well my old mum is going to have to catch a bus because of you. And her hips are held together with metal pins.'

'Jesus.'

Chester's tapping fingers came through down the line. 'Look,' he said, as though he was passing on a secret. 'It's a sure thing, Jack. You should put some money on it, too. Eddie popped in over the weekend and dropped the tip. All he wanted for it was a Dick Francis hardcover. I slipped in an old paperback for him, too.'

'Christ,' said Jack, tiredness weighing him down like a chain-mail shirt.

'Eddie's out there all day. Take you five minutes.'

Eddie Roy. He was about a hundred years old, dressed like it was still 1932, and sold thin, grilled sausages from a greasy cart at Royal Randwick. He apparently owned a little corner of a large turd that had been dropped by Phar Lap, in which he read the future, like it was tea leaves. He had picked a few long shots in his time and a kind of myth had swirled up around him. With the human tendency to want to believe in the miraculous, Eddie Roy had done all right. Apparently his father had been some kind of preacher. Now the true believers, the miracle chasers, went to the track and not to church.

'Race six,' said Chester. 'Babylon Boy, fifty on the nose. You got it?'

Jack scribbled it down. 'Yeah, I got it.'

'The car's parked round at my place. White Subaru with roof-racks.'

'Keys?'

'You don't need them. Any key is fine. Number ten, Cary Street, Leichhardt.'

'Sure it's still there?'

'Nobody *knows* any key will do.'

'What else is wrong with it?'

'Nothing. But there's no petrol in it at the moment.'

Jack closed his eyes, craned his head back. 'What about wheels, Sinclair? Do I need to bring my own?'

'Just the petrol. And watch it on the corners. The front left brake bites and pulls round hard. I nearly wiped out a pedestrian the other day.'

'Maybe I'll take my neighbour's bike.'

'And have it back by six.'

'Will it last that long?'

'The car is pure finesse and Japanese reliability, Susko. Never let me down.'

Jack grunted.

'Full tank, plus fifty,' repeated Sinclair. 'Babylon Boy with Eddie, back by six. You crash, you pay.' Chester hung up.

Jack put the phone down. On the counter, among the small pile of books he had rescued from the floor, *The Art of War* by Sun Tzu: Denma translation, Shambhala Classics, Boston, USA, fourth edition. That was more like it. How to kick some *ass*. He closed his eyes, opened the book. Threw a thought at his predicament and then put his finger down. Looked. Page 21.

Subtle! Subtle!
To the point of formlessness.
Spiritlike! Spiritlike!
To the point of soundlessness.
Thus one can be the enemy's fate star.

Jack tossed the book back onto the counter. Gathered his things. He was going to need something a little more precise than that. Something a little more *how to*.

~18~

PARRAMATTA ROAD WAS HOT AND UNPLEASANT AS USUAL. Lined with empty shops like an old film set, only traffic rushing by. The route 440 bus Jack had caught was one of the old, non-air-conditioned numbers, and even though all the windows were open and the roof vents were up and there were only four people creating body heat, Jack was sweating himself into a stupor inside the metal box. Out on the horizon there were more glimpses of thick clouds rising high into the air, brewing rain for a storm. Jack hoped it would hit soon.

He got off on the corner of Norton and Marion streets. Passenger jets roared overhead, adding to the rumble of buses and cars, and to the heavy heat that just sat on everything, dusty and low and brown. Sinclair's place was around the corner. Jack found the car about three doors down: a white, 1992 Subaru Fiori, rusted to within an inch of its life.

It was about the size of a box of matches. Driving it would be the equivalent of strapping a saddle to a fruit fly. Jack looked through the window: books, papers, magazines, empty Snickers wrappers and Pepsi Max cans, takeaway coffee cups, a weary cardboard box on the back seat with the arm of a black jumper draped over it. Darth Vader hanging from the rear-view mirror. He pulled open the driver's side door and nearly fell over: close to a thousand degrees in there. Strong smell of kebab, garlicky baba ganoush, stale sweat. As Jack worked his way into the seat and wound the window down, he seriously contemplated walking to Bankstown. It was as though he had climbed into Chester Sinclair's armpit.

Jack used the key to his apartment: the motor kicked over. Seven hundred and fifty-eight cubic centimetres of pure power at his fingertips. Nought to one hundred in three weeks. By the time Jack had filled up the tank and was rolling down Old Canterbury Road, he had discovered that nothing worked except the warning lights: every single one glowed bright red. Maybe the thing was about to explode? Or maybe the car was psychic, telling Jack to beware of approaching doom?

Bankstown shimmered with heat. The glare made Jack squint. Old Canterbury Road had eventually led the Fiori into a suburb of wide, low streets lined with single-storey dwellings and warehouses, and parched, empty allotments.

Jack drove through, into the shopping streets, past parks and playgrounds, eventually turning into Begonia Place. Somewhere that he had not been in too many years to remember.

Cousin Carl's house was a low, orange brick-veneer place with a dark-brown tiled roof and peeling brown aluminium guttering. There was a large, bare front yard of dry, patchy grass, its centrepiece a deflated red-and-white wading pool, full of leaves and a couple of drowned toys. On the right, a concrete driveway with an oily nature strip down the middle: it led to a pole-framed carport where a dented, grimy white van was parked. An air-conditioning unit strapped to the side of the house vibrated roughly.

The place had not changed much. Jack walked up to the front door, nervous, thinking about cigarettes, thinking about how it had been a very long time since he last made his way across this scrappy lawn to spend the afternoon with his Aunt Eva. Dropped off without a word but with five bucks for a drink and an ice cream down at the shops. An old feeling stirred in the sludge of his memory, like a sleeping crocodile shifting in thick mud. Regret? Anger? Guilt? Maybe a little of everything. Even happiness. Aunt Eva had always been good to him.

He knocked on the metal frame of the screen door, the sound flimsy, like the splash and rattle of aluminium foil. After a moment, he heard somebody moving around inside and waited. He looked over his shoulder, out into the broad bright street. Nostalgia always made him nauseous. Somebody ought to invent a procedure where you could drain it off and bottle it and shoot it into outer space. Most times, Jack reckoned the past was a pointless exercise.

'Can I help you?'

A woman looked through the screen door. She had messy, shoulder-length ash-blonde hair, tucked in behind her ears, and tired hazel eyes in a tired tanned face. Early forty-something, though probably younger in fact. She wore a white singlet and pale-pink shorts, barefoot with a tea towel in her hand. Her toenails were painted red. There was a two-year-old clinging to her leg. The woman had a small, rounded body, soft-fleshed and a little post-baby plump, but shapely and smooth brown. Attractive, but needed a week off, just her and a lot of sleep. Her left hand rested on the child's shoulder. She was smiling and it was like a warm backlight in her face; Jack saw that she was one of the world's troopers, weary but trying to be happy, and getting there, slowly.

'Hi,' he said, returning her smile. 'I'm Carl's cousin, Jack Susko.'

She pressed her lips together and gave a small look of pain, as though the two-year-old had pinched her. 'Oh.'

'Is he in?'

'Um, no. He's out. On a job.'

Jack noticed the warmth in her face fading. 'Back soon?'

'Um … no. I don't know.' Behind her, another child, four, maybe five, appeared in the hallway, holding on to the doorjamb, peering out, his face glum.

'Look, I don't want to —'

'I'm really sorry,' said the woman, reaching to give the back of the little boy against her leg a rub. 'I know he should have returned it by now, but he still needs the car.'

'Right.'

'The van,' she said, unsure, and nodded towards the

carport. 'It's no good.'

Jack glanced down at the boy. He had his mother's ash-blonde hair, round cheeks and brow; his father's small eyes and sharp nose. 'Yeah,' said Jack. 'Carl mentioned something.'

'Mum …' The other boy stepped into the hallway behind his mother. 'I'm hungry.'

'Yes darling. In a minute.' She looked at Jack, her face meek, a touch flushed and embarrassed.

Jack tucked the edge of a grin into his cheek. He wanted to put the woman at ease. 'We can sort the car out later. But I need to speak to Carl.'

Her face unburdened, relaxed a little. Somewhere in the house, a baby began crying. The woman straightened up, gave a here-we-go-again roll of her eyes. 'Won't be a second.' She went down the hall and then through a door on her right. The two-year-old scurried along after her, calling 'Mummy, Mummy, Mummy', dragging a small, worn-looking length of blue flannelette behind him. The older boy remained where he was and watched Jack from under the fringe of his blond hair.

'How's it going?' Jack shifted his feet, uneasy before the boy's unblinking gaze. He pulled what he thought was a friendly face. The kid stared, did not move, said nothing.

'That's great.' The kid was starting to freak him out a little. *Jesus.* In the penetrating high beam of his eyes, it was as though Jack had done something wrong.

The woman came back, a baby in her arms. Pink, plump wrists and cheeks and feet, everything bursting with chubbiness. Crystal blue eyes, narrowed and unfocused and bemused, almost annoyed, like the kid was over the world already. The two-year-old trailed behind, holding on to the hem of his mother's shorts.

'Got any more?' said Jack.

She smiled. 'No. Just the three.' She held the baby up in the nook of her arm. 'This is Amelia. Our little surprise. Weren't you, darling?'

'Must keep you nice and busy.'

She gave him a look of exasperation. 'Uh-huh. Just a bit.' Her rounded shoulders slumped slightly.

'So Carl will be back tonight, then?' Jack remembered why he was there. Waiting until tonight to give his cousin one in the guts, maybe two, was not something he wanted to do.

'Look, um, no. Probably not.' The woman adjusted the child, bounced it slightly like a stack of weekend newspapers too heavy on her arm. Her face darkened and some kind of pain sucked in her cheeks. She glanced behind her, then leaned a little towards Jack, spoke in a softer voice. 'Carl's at a friend's place. We're … we're having a break for a while.' She closed her eyes for a moment, squeezed them hard, held back whatever it was that wanted to spill freely from her. Her neck flushed and her eyes were glazed when she opened them again.

'Mum?'

'It's all right, darling.' With great skill, a happy, unconcerned face slipped into place, like a holiday slide, clicked into a projector's beaming light. She smiled at Jack.

'Do you know where he's staying?' Jack felt seriously awkward.

She nodded quickly, turned to the older boy behind her. 'Toby, could you get Uncle Jack a drink from the kitchen, please. There's a ginger beer in the fridge.'

Uncle Jack. He had never heard that one before.

'That's my ginger beer.'

'Mummy'll get you some more. Please, darling.'

'Just a glass of water is fine.'

'It's all right. Come on, Toby. Skip to it.'

The woman reached out and pushed open the screen door. Held out her free hand. 'I'm Renée, by the way.'

'Hello, Renée.'

'And this is Nicholas. Say hello, darling.'

Nicholas turned his face and pressed it into his mother's soft brown thigh. Renée tousled his hair. 'Come on, shy boy.'

'No!'

'Oh, grumpy bum …'

Toby came back, handing his mother a half-glass of water. 'Here.'

'Say hello to Uncle Jack.'

'No.' He walked off and disappeared through a door.

'Sorry,' said Renée. She looked down at her youngest.

'Don't worry about it.'

Renée closed her eyes for a moment. Her forehead sweaty and flushed. Then she glanced up and smiled another apology, creased the skin in all the small corners of her face. She handed Jack the glass of water. 'I'll try and speak to Carl.'

Young Nicholas turned his head slightly and peeked up. 'Sure,' said Jack. For a moment he wondered if she was talking about Carl busting up Susko Books. He drank the water.

'So do you know where Carl's staying?'

'Friends in Surry Hills,' she said, with a look of disgust. It quickly changed to anger. 'His *actor* friends. I don't know the address. And I couldn't give a shit.' Renée looked out past Jack into the street, rubbing the young boy's shoulder a little harder.

The skin around Jack's skull tightened. 'Actors?'

'Losers. They've convinced Carl that he's got talent. Ha!' She stopped, gathering her self-control.

'What was the name of — '

'He's a father of three, for God's sake!' Renée was not listening. 'Not to mention a husband.' The kid looked up at his mother, his eyes big and round and wet.

'You know,' continued Renée, 'I saw them all in a play once. Oh, yes. And you know what? It was embarrassing! Just terrible.' She looked down, ruffled her boy's hair. 'It was pathetic. Better actors at my son's school.'

'Can you remember the theatre?'

'Palomino or something,' she replied. 'The *effing* Palomino.'

Same as Larissa. Same as Shane.

'The *bastard*.'

Awkwardness worked its way between them again. Jack had no idea how to respond: thought that he should say sorry, or something, but said nothing.

Renée let out a large breath and a long sigh.

Jack handed over the glass of water, gave her a sympathetic smile. 'Thanks for that. I'd better make a move.' He took one step backwards, down from the small area of concrete in front of the door, onto the curved, cracked path that led to the street. Blue and red chalk was scrawled here and there, nondescript drawings only the boys could decipher. 'Look, if you do see or hear from Carl, could you tell him to call me?' he said.

Renée closed her eyes again and nodded, moving back into the house and closing the security door at the same time. She disappeared behind its shadowy, flyscreen darkness. Jack held up a hand and moved off, back across the hot, scrappy lawn, towards the Fiori parked down the street.

It did not start first go. Or on the second or on the third, but that was not what had suddenly begun to annoy Jack. Nor was it the cramped interior and sauna-level temperature. It was Lewis the bodyguard in the de Groot Maserati, parked about a hundred metres behind him down the road, trying to look inconspicuous among the Fords and Mazdas and Hyundais, which combined were probably worth about the same as the leather trim on the Maserati's steering wheel.

Son of a bitch. Now they were following him?

The Fiori moaned and squealed and finally started. Jack pulled out, eyes flashing to the rear-view mirror as he watched for traffic. There was somebody in the passenger side of the Maserati, too, but he could not see who it was. He wondered whether Chester would mind if he got up a little speed and rammed the Subaru into de Groot's wheels. Jack was tempted, but knew he could do more damage with a full can of Pepsi.

He drove off. Glanced over at his bag on the seat beside him. Three-point-four-million-dollar postal slip inside.

Jack had noticed before that Lewis had trouble moving his head left and right. Too many muscles in the neck. Maybe if Jack took a few sharp corners, he might lose him.

~*19*~

As far as Jack was aware, the Subaru Fiori had never featured as a getaway car, on film or on the page: but he quickly discovered the hidden talents of Chester Sinclair's little shit box. Two, in fact. Firstly, the car was difficult to see in traffic — especially from the low, slinky driving position behind the wheel of a Maserati Quattroporte; and secondly, it could be driven down laneways barely wide enough for mothers with prams. What the Fiori lacked in style and power, it made up for with cunning. Just like an old, arthritic rat.

Jack drove back up Old Canterbury Road, then criss-crossed Parramatta Road, heading for the city. He wound through Glebe and Annandale, swung over into Newtown and drove through the narrow streets, eyes flicking nervously up to the rear-view mirror. He could feel Lewis' arm around his neck. The bodyguard kept up for a while in the fancy Italian wheels, just a few cars back, but by the time Jack slipped down a couple of bin-lined rear lanes in Redfern, his tail was free. He drove to Susko Books in a hurry. Chester could wait.

He came to York Street, turned the Fiori down Market Row, and parked right outside the rear door to Susko Books. It was a prime tow-away area. Jack flicked the hazard lights on and wrote a note that he left on the dashboard: *Delivery — if need car moved, pls ask at desk, Susko Books.*

Jack unlocked the door and entered the shop. Books still all over the floor. What next? He stood there, thinking. Heart beating. He felt as though he had walked into his own head. Everybody wanted what he had and everybody knew where he was. Maybe the first thing to do was make himself less accessible. That was a start. But where?

A tap on the window outside made him look up. Kim Archer waved at Jack from behind the glass, smiling. Jack held up his hand and walked over to let her in. Some of the tension in his body eased.

'Hi,' she said, face bright and shiny with a thin film of sweat. 'Boy, it's a stinker out there!'

'Welcome to my cavern of cool. Just don't mind the mess.'

Kim took in the space. 'What happened?'

'Stocktake sale,' said Jack, letting Kim in and then locking the door behind her. 'They always go nuts.'

'Really?' She looked around, hands on hips. 'Do they buy anything or just throw it around?'

'Mostly throw it around. It's the new retail therapy.'

She grinned, turned her dark-brown eyes onto Jack. The faintest tint of blue around them. Nude lips shining, her white-blonde hair soft and brushed messily forwards. She was wearing leopard-skin tights and a baggy black T-shirt with a 1950s Elvis Presley on the front in white. Red Converse sneakers and a shiny gold handbag in the shape of a clam, the thin strap across her body. Expensive-smelling perfume and a general air of cheekiness. Kim Archer grew on Jack a little more.

'Seriously,' she said. 'Did somebody do the place over?'

Jack nodded.

'My God! Have you called the police?'

'They said they'd get here sometime in January. Afternoon, most likely.'

Kim continued to look around, stunned. 'Did they take anything?'

'Probably.'

'You've got to call the police.'

'Don't worry, I have.'

She frowned at him, unsure. 'I don't believe you.'

Jack pulled a sad, serious face. Walked to the counter. 'Then we have no future together.'

When he turned around, he saw Kim's mouth stretched wide, clean white teeth glowing through her lips. She picked up a couple of books from the floor and brought them over to the counter.

'I've always wanted to work in a bookshop,' she said.

'You can start today. Five bucks an hour and all the books you can eat.'

'Done.'

Jack's knees felt a little oiled. 'So, you're here for a book?' He scratched his chin. 'I'd say ... *Charlotte's Web*.'

Kim grinned, pleased. 'Very good. You could also add *A Thousand Things to Do on a Rainy Day*.'

'Ah, yes,' said Jack. 'Now I see it all. What else?'

'Well, actually, Shane sent me to pick up a book for *him*.'

Jack held his breath for a moment.

'Said you'd know all about it.'

'Right.'

Kim looked at him, a little confused. 'Don't you?'

'Yeah.' Jack cleared his throat. 'I know about it. Is he back?'

'No, still in China. He said it was a gift for someone and could I send it for him.'

'Who's the lucky person?'

'Larissa someone, I can't remember her last name. She's a friend of Shane's. I met her a couple of times at the house.'

Jack nodded.

'What's the book?' asked Kim. 'Shane didn't tell me.'

'A little Bible.'

'Really? She didn't look like the religious type to me.'

'Evangelical Christian, apparently.'

'Right.' Kim crouched to the floor and gathered up a few more books. 'Anyway, it's nice of Shane. He's never bought me a thing.'

Jesus. Jack wondered where Shane actually was. Obviously being beaten up was no deterrent to the unemployed actor. Then again, three-and-a-bit mill was pretty hard to resist: especially if it had slipped through your hands once already.

'Shane does a bit of theatre stuff, too, doesn't he?' he asked.

'On and off. Actually he was in a play ... when was it? Last month?' Kim raised her eyebrows. 'Shane was ... okay.'

'Where?'

'The Palomino. Not far from our place, just down on Devonshire Street. They did Molière: *Le Malade Imaginaire*.'

'Know your seventeenth-century comic dramatists then?'

'The costumes were shit. The elastic on Shane's eye-mask snapped in the middle of a scene.'

'Really?' Jack hoped it had stung. 'Know any of the other actors?'

'Oh, a couple. Why?'

'I was wondering if it was the same one my cousin was in.'

'What's his name?'

'Carl,' said Jack. 'Carl Reiss.'

Kim's face brightened. 'Carl Reiss is your cousin? Really?'

'You know him?'

'Yeah, he's friends with Shane as well. He comes around all the time. He's really sweet.'

'Like a tray of baklava.'

Kim brushed book dust from her hands. 'Isn't that funny? He's your cousin!'

'Hilarious.'

'You don't like him?'

'I don't think so, no.'

She went to say something else but pointed over Jack's shoulder instead. 'Somebody wants to buy a book.'

Jack turned. There was a face up to the glass of the door. Hands cupped around the eyes, peering in. A big, tall guy.

Kim checked her watch. 'Are you closed?'

Jack grabbed her by the wrist. 'Come on,' he said, pulling

her towards the rear door. 'We've got to go.'

'Hey, what —'

'*Now.*'

She stumbled as she turned but let herself be led. Jack stopped at the back door and released her arm. He listened for a second, then gave Kim what he hoped was a sincere look. 'Sorry I grabbed you like that,' he said, voice low and serious. 'But that guy isn't my long-lost twin separated at birth. Know what I mean?'

Kim nodded, pulled the strap of her bag further up her shoulder. Her freckles had faded to the barest tint of light brown.

'Best if you just walk normally down the lane and back round to York Street or wherever you're going. Look like you're on your way somewhere. He doesn't know you so there's nothing to worry about. Okay?'

Her face tightened. 'What are you going to do?'

'Take my super-car for a run.' He enjoyed her momentary tone of concern. Lately, it had only been Jack Susko worrying about Jack Susko.

'I'll come with you,' she said.

Jack did not answer. He held the door to Susko Books open a crack and peered into Market Row. Nobody there. He turned to Kim and ushered her through. 'Right. Off you go.'

She stepped out but then stopped and blocked the way. 'No,' she said. 'Give me a lift.'

Jack was right up against her now, trying to close the door behind him. The Fiori wedged them together into the narrow space, between building and car. Jack twisted himself up a little and pulled the handle. The door clicked shut.

They heard running footsteps approach the nearest corner. Kim grabbed the car door. 'Get in!' she said, firmly. Her tone sounded a little too much like she was enjoying herself. She jumped into the car, reached across and popped the driver's side door open.

Jack ran around. As he reached the door, he saw Pascal swing into the lane, leaning like a motorbike on the apex, then head full pelt straight at him.

Shit. He pulled keys out of his pocket and pushed one into the ignition. *Shit.* The Fiori moaned, whirred, but did not kick. *Come on.* Jack glanced up: Pascal was getting bigger in the rear-view mirror. Ignition again. The car clicked, then squealed.

'Hurry up, Jack.'

'Yeah, I *know* —'

The car kicked over. Jack dropped the clutch and took off down Market Row. The Fiori could probably just beat a three-legged poodle, but anything else was out of its league. Jack checked the rear-view mirror again. He hoped Pascal was not as fit as he looked.

~20~

NOT THAT IT MATTERED.

Up ahead, Kablunak's Mercedes swung into the lane, illegally. Hazard lights flashing. It stopped a few metres in. Jack slammed the brakes and the Fiori came to a soggy stop. Hazard lights flashing, too. Nobody moved for a moment. Engines idled in hot Market Row. Jack gripped the thin steering wheel, stared at the darkened windscreen of the Mercedes. He revved the Fiori's toy engine. The Mercedes revved back. A face-off. Between a tsunami and a gumnut.

'What's that guy doing?' asked Kim, irritated that her excitement had ended prematurely.

'Winning,' said Jack.

Pascal came up the side of the Fiori and opened the

driver's side door. 'Hey, Jack.' He leaned in and switched off the motor. 'Out you get.'

Jack turned to Kim. 'Wait here.' He got out of the car. Pascal walked him over to the Mercedes. The tinted front passenger window slid down, silently. It stopped just past halfway. Viktor Kablunak's face was behind it.

'Hello, Jack,' said the Russian, sunglasses on, dark hair slicked, crisp white collars on a crisp white shirt. 'It is hot today, no? Let's go for a ride. I want to buy you a gelato.' Behind the shades, his face gave nothing away.

'Thanks. But I'm diabetic.'

'Get in,' said Pascal.

'I can't leave my car there.'

'Tell your friend to take it away.'

The Russian turned to Pascal. 'Check the car, first.'

'You still don't believe me, Viktor? I told you I haven't got it.'

Kablunak stared straight ahead.

Jack shrugged, looked at Kim. She held up her hands — *what's going on?* — then rested an elbow on the windowsill. Smiled. Somehow, the gravity of the situation had not hit her. She still looked like she was having fun.

Pascal searched the car. A minute or so later, he shook his head at Kablunak in the Mercedes.

'Say goodbye, Mr Susko.'

Jack walked back to the Fiori. Crouched down beside the open, driver's side door. 'You drive?'

Kim nodded.

'All right if you take the Ferrari back to your place?'

'Sure.'

'I'll pick it up there later.'

Her face tightened with concern. 'Are you okay? Should I call the police?'

'No, it's fine. Just going for a chat. Nothing to worry about.'

'Are you sure?'

Jack smiled. 'Careful in this thing,' he said. 'It's powerful.'

'Hey … have you got a phone?'

'Yeah, I do.' Jack tapped the mobile in his pocket. It was not a bad idea. He pulled out his wallet and handed Kim a card. 'My number's on there. Call if you don't hear from me in a week or two.'

Jack walked back to the Mercedes. The rear passenger door opened with a thick, expensive-luxury-car sound. He glanced at his own reflection for a second, distorted in the dark curved glass, and climbed in. Pascal followed on the other side and sat across from him on the back seat. Walter was behind the wheel. He backed the car out of Market Row, ignoring traffic, and took off down the street.

They hit the exit ramp for Anzac Bridge.

'So what have you guys been up to today?' said Jack, trying not to think about where they might be taking him. 'Beach? Barbecue at a friend's house?'

No answer. Kablunak reached over for the controls on the car audio system and turned the volume up. There were enough buttons there to manoeuvre a small satellite into position. It was probably what he had just done. The sound from the stereo was deep and round and the music seemed to be coming out of everywhere. Slow, smooth trumpet filled the Mercedes to the brim.

Jack listened, a little surprised. It was Dizzy Gillespie. 'Cocktails for Two'.

'Is that the Paris recording?' asked Jack, forgetting for a moment that he might be in serious physical danger.

'Théâtre des Champs-Elysées,' said Kablunak, in pretty good French. 'March 25, 1952. Do you know it, Mr Susko?'

'Sure. Don Byas on tenor sax, Art Simmons on piano, Joe Benjamin on double bass, Bill Clark on drums.'

Kablunak turned a little of his profile towards Jack and held up a manicured finger. 'And Humberto Canto Morales on congas,' he said.

'Not on this track.'

Kablunak nodded. 'So, you know something, Mr Susko.'

'Sometimes,' said Jack.

'Excellent. Then there is a good chance we will understand one another.'

Walter indicated and changed into the right lane to pass a bus, indicated and swung back again into the left. It was tight with traffic, all red brake lights down the line. Jack could see him in the rear-view mirror, grimacing through the jazz.

'Dizzy Gillespie is in my top five of the best trumpeters ever,' said Kablunak. 'Do you —' The track stopped and he held up his hand. 'Wait. Listen.'

Now 'Moon Nocturne' spilled in around them. Like floating in heaven. Jack saw Fat Boy close his eyes for a moment, as though suffering a toothache. Pascal looked out of the window.

'My God,' said Kablunak. His fingers played his thigh. 'A genius.'

Jack nodded, but not too much. 'Sure is.'

The Russian watched a couple of motorcycles weave through the traffic. 'And you, Jack?' he said. 'Who would make your top five?'

'Wouldn't know where to start.'

Viktor Kablunak shook his head. 'Do not be so boring. Okay, yes, you are right, it is a stupid question. A game. Who is the best, who is your favourite, what is your top five of all time, yes. It does not tell the whole truth. But conversation is … too *abstract*, in the beginning. We start somewhere because it is necessary to start. No? Am I making sense to you, Jack?'

'Can I think about it for a minute?'

'*Bah*. All I mean is that I see you like jazz. This is just a start. We must move around one another. A first coordinate. A simple question. I would like to know you better, Jack.'

'Sure.'

'But you do not wish to indulge me with an answer?'

'You think we can be friends, Viktor?'

'I see.' Kablunak was thoughtful for a moment. 'Yes. We have not met under normal circumstances. That is a problem.'

As comfortable as it was in the Mercedes, Jack was moving swiftly towards discomfort and unease, like a kid about to hit a muddy puddle at the end of the slippery slide.

'I was fifteen,' said Kablunak, spreading himself in the seat, tugging at the ironed creases of his pale-grey pants. 'Living in the Soviet Union' — he waved a hand above his shoulder — 'Nowhere. Living. A kind of life. I heard Duke Ellington.' He paused, apparently lost for words. 'Glorious. Free. A black man soaring high above the clouds. Do you understand, Mr Susko?'

'Uh-huh,' said Jack, his tongue thick and dry. He understood that Viktor Kablunak liked an audience.

'It was my revelation. My ... *revolution*. Because of Duke Ellington, I found a home in America.'

Jack remembered Kablunak mentioning the Russian border deal with the Chinese that had displaced his family. 'Where?'

He patted his chest, firmly, twice. 'Here.'

Jack glanced at Walter and Pascal: from the looks on their faces, he guessed they had heard this before.

'Music is a parallel universe,' the Russian continued. 'There are no limits, no ... restrictions, on who a man is, who a man can be. Music is pure energy. Man is simply just the wire along which it runs.' Kablunak turned towards Jack again, twisting his head half around. 'Freedom, you see? Freedom.'

Jack nodded, wanting a little of that freedom himself right now.

'But free only while playing the music. Free while they play, because when they play, they *are* music. Not men anymore. But' — this time he held up his forefinger, waved it like a school teacher at a student, accusingly — 'we all, eventually, must return to our minds. And so to our identities. To our histories and our geographies. To be judged by *inferior* minds. To be imprisoned in ways worse than the worst gulag. To be held against our will in untruths and falseness.' He lowered his voice. 'By men made of mud.'

'You get all that from Duke Ellington?'

Kablunak did not reply. He patted Walter on the thigh. His driver flinched. 'Don't forget I need to post a letter.'

His tubby driver nodded. He swung the Mercedes off Anzac Bridge and followed Victoria Road.

'Where are we going?'

'Just a drive, Mr Susko. So we can talk.'

'About jazz?'

Kablunak nodded.

'What about the blues? That's more the mood I'm in.'

Kablunak reached over to the audio controls again and pressed a couple of buttons. Dizzy went away and silence padded out the inside of the Merc. Not even a flutter from the speakers. A moment later, a loud hissing and scratching: something old, digitised and compressed into a CD, but forever grained with its own time. Acoustic guitar, stripped and bare. Played on a knife-edge and true as a pummelling, straight-line train. Jack felt the warmth of recognition. Robert Johnson, riding the rhythm, sweat stinging his eyes. Resigned to his fate and getting there fast.

If I had possession, over Judgement Day
If I had possession, over Judgement Day
Lord, the little woman I'm lovin' wouldn't
Have no right to pray

Kablunak turned the music down a touch. 'I know what it is to be a black man, Mr Susko,' he said, eyes on the road in front of them. 'Like nothing, like a lump of man, treated without dignity or respect. Treated worse than a dog.' He brushed his pants and then rested his hands on his thighs, continued looking through the windscreen. 'The terror of no escape from your condition. The hell of being chained to a post in the ground while everybody around you walks this way and that, driven by whim.' He paused for a moment. 'I am from Russian peasants, Mr Susko. From nothing. I know what it is to be a black man.'

Walter approached a set of lights, got the green arrow straight away and turned the big car right. They drove slowly along Darling Street, under a green canopy of plane trees, still lit golden by the late-afternoon sun. A slightly wind-twisted banner stretched across as well, strung between the buildings on either side, announcing a school fête. Jack shifted in his seat, the leather creaking lightly beneath him. The outside world seemed unreal and distant. A little like the world inside the car, only nowhere near as menacing.

Had to fold my arms and I, slowly walked away
Had to fold my arms and I, slowly walked away
I said in my mind
'Your trouble gonna come some day'

Viktor Kablunak sat and listened to the music and felt the smoothness of his chin with his fingertips.

'I told you I still haven't got the Sergius,' said Jack. 'You searched the car, the shop. What's with the ride?'

Kablunak took his time answering. 'I fear temptation, Mr Susko. It is around every corner, hidden in every shadow. Waiting to *pounce*.'

'Sounds like you need God, Viktor. I really can't help you with that.'

'Oh, no, Jack. It is *your* temptation I fear. It has come to my attention that others, too, know of the Sergius and its ... unfortunate redirection out of my hands.' A pause. 'Into yours.'

Jack frowned. *Larissa?* Kablunak surely knew. Shane would hardly have endured any more beatings to keep her name out of it.

'Maybe you underestimate my desire to get out of this situation as quickly as possible,' said Jack. He glanced over at Pascal beside him.

'Really?' Kablunak grinned. 'I personally do not know anybody who rushes out of situations that might be worth millions of dollars to them.'

'What's worth millions of dollars, Viktor?' Jack hoped he sounded like he had no idea what Kablunak was talking about.

'I think that is obvious, Mr Susko. Even if you do not know what the Sergius is worth, you know it is worth *something*. And besides, I have essentially just told you. Do not play the fool with me.' The Russian looked out the window. 'There is already enough foolishness with Richard de Groot.'

Jack exhaled slowly. The air-conditioning inside the Mercedes was moving from comfortable to chilly. He swallowed a little nervousness down. 'What's the story with de Groot?'

Viktor Kablunak scoffed, then laughed, lightly. 'A fool's story.'

'Can you be more specific?'

'There is only one fool's story. It is as old as man's vanity. Details are irrelevant.'

'I heard you were old friends. What happened? Did Dicky get the girl?'

'The girl, Mr Susko?' Kablunak shook his head. 'No. He, of all people, should know what I am capable of.' His voice was not too loud, not too soft, and about as friendly as a serial killer asking for your home address. 'He does not understand ... *things*.'

'What kind of things?'

'Capitalism has always been about survival of the fittest. Competition,' said Kablunak, as though he had not heard Jack's question. 'What makes Richard think that only *he* does not need to suffer it?' The volume of his voice rose along the length of the sentence. 'Pieces of shit like him, who have always had everything, who have trodden on the black man for so long. Apartheid! Hah! And now they cry, up and down Double Bay and Rose Bay and Vaucluse. *The Russians are coming! The Russians are coming!*' Kablunak pulled out a folded, pale-blue handkerchief from his pocket and dabbed at his mouth. He regained his composure. 'He must understand. Even if there is no *borscht* on the menus in the cafés, I am *here*. And I am not going away.'

Jack looked at Walter, then turned to Pascal. Both continued to maintain the same blank faces as before. The smart money seemed to be on *no comment*.

They drove through Balmain. The sky was fattening with storm clouds and shadows passed over the car. Kablunak stared out the window; in the reflection on the glass, Jack could see that his mouth was one muscle flick away from a snarl. The Russian flexed his fingers; wiggled them a little, like he was about to roll some dice. He curled his thumb around the forefinger and clicked the knuckle.

'How we degenerate, Mr Susko,' he said, breaking the silence. 'How we decline. Entropy of the body. Of the spirit. Of dignity.' Kablunak nodded to himself. 'And the real difference between men? Only time. Some get there sooner. Some later. We should always remember that it is death that defines us. Yes, the darkness.' Now he shook his head, sadly. 'You will have yours and I will have mine. Are you prepared, Mr Susko? It is important not to be afraid.'

Jack needed some air. He cleared his throat, breathed hard through his nostrils. A little feeling had gone from his right leg and he tried to squeeze some back into it. 'So how do you rate Coltrane's sax?' he asked.

Viktor Kablunak laughed; his shoulders bounced lightly for a moment. 'Ah, maybe you are wise, Mr Susko,' he said. 'It is true. Philosophy is a downward spiral to depression and anxiety and ... *nothingness*. Much better to live and die, than to think and die.'

'Okay Viktor, how's this? One hundred thousand for the Sergius. That'd leave you more than enough change. And compensate me for all the stress. And lead me not into temptation.'

'But deliver you from evil?' Kablunak showed Jack his profile. 'I like you, Mr Susko. A man of action. But do not let yourself get too ... *spontaneous*.'

'I like you, too, Viktor. That's why I'm giving you right of first refusal.'

The Russian yawned. 'I will explain it to you, Mr Susko. So that there is no confusion.'

They had reached the end of Darling Street, a bus turning circle down on the water in Balmain East. With the harbour and the bridge and the city across from them, turning grey beneath the looming storm. Walter turned right into a narrow lane between two large sandstone buildings. He came to a nature reserve and swung the

Mercedes into the gravel car park. He stopped, facing the harbour. Turned the engine off. Nobody else around.

Kablunak stared out at the water and the city, silver and darkening steel. 'I do not wish to spoil our new friendship, Mr Susko. But, you understand, I must apply some … *pressure* to this situation.'

'All right. Fifty thousand. A bargain.' Jack's tone was coming in a little high and squeaky. A small wave of panic pinned-and-needled his back.

'Please. I give you credit for some intelligence. So. Learn this lesson now and you will be your own man.' Kablunak looked through the windscreen: self-assured, complete, like a king. He continued to gaze at the harbour, which now seemed huge, foreground and background at the same time, rising up. 'There is pleasure,' he said. 'And there is business. Once it was called war and peace. But only labels change. What was there before is there still.'

Pascal jammed a gun into Jack's side. 'Out you pop,' he said.

Jack climbed out of the car, followed by Pascal. It was still hot and humid, but a light breeze blew in off the harbour. Jack breathed, deeply. He walked, a little shaky on his feet. Pascal led him down the grass slope towards a children's play area. It was a small, compact set-up. Slides and swings, monkey bars and tunnels. Empty right now. Not a single five-year-old in sight, ready to jump in for the rescue.

Jack noticed how the horizon seemed to have curled up and over the city, like a giant wave of thick, blackening smoke, frozen at the peak of its swelling. The dark storm was working its way in. Time to get out of the way.

'So,' said Viktor Kablunak behind him. 'I must now put

my mark on you, Mr Susko.'

'You've gone to a lot of trouble, Viktor. Why didn't you just beat me up back at the shop?'

'And where would the ritual be, Mr Susko? The symbolism? Life is but a series of small, insignificant ... *gestures*. Thrown to the wind. But men were made for acts of faith and courage. And death! We must try and infuse all of our actions with the quality of myth, to give them meaning beyond the mere action of them. To lift us out of banality and to liberate us from death!' The Russian paused. 'We must be grand, Mr Susko, or we are nothing. Do not succumb to the evil of ... *efficiency*.'

'Sounds good, Viktor. I think you've made your point.'

'I can hear fear in your voice, Mr Susko. Good. I am satisfied. And hopefully, you are convinced of my serious nature.'

Before Jack could say anything else, something hit him in the head. He thought it must have been one of the buildings in the city falling down, right across the water and on top of the children's play area. But he never found out for sure. The world switched off like a plasma TV. Nothing. Blackness. Cold.

~21~

A FIVE-YEAR-OLD KID FOUND HIM LYING across the small slatted bridge of the children's fort. He ran to get his mummy. Jack blinked. It was painful, so he stopped doing it, kept his eyes closed. Groaned instead. As he came to, it was a bumpy ride. He remembered what had happened. Right away, his head felt like a thousand hangovers after an afternoon of brain surgery. He opened his eyes: it even hurt to *look*.

The mother came back with the child. Jack tried to speak, mumbled, moaned, made no sense. The mother told him that it was disgusting, a grown man drunk in a children's playground, and as she walked off, child in hand, she said she was calling the police.

Jack carefully felt the back of his head. Bump about the

size of a mango. Pulsing and hot. He changed his mind. *Baked potato.*

After what felt like an hour, he sat up. He thought he might vomit but managed to keep his guts down. He got to his feet. Jack wondered if he should go to hospital: have himself checked out? Maybe. But his vision was losing the blur, so he took it as a good sign. Maybe it all just felt worse than it actually was. More important to get back to Susko Books and grab the postal slip before anybody else did. Nobody was getting nothing for nothing anymore.

On the bus, Jack tried Larissa's number. All he got was her recorded voice, bright and confident: *Hi there. I can't come to the phone right now, but if you leave your name and number, I'll get back to you as soon as possible. Thanks!*

Jack waited for the beep. Had he really trusted her? Was that what had stung him?

Maybe.

'Larissa. It's Jack. Three-point-four million, huh? It must have just slipped your mind.'

He ended the call. Slid low in the seat and carefully rested his head back.

Rhonda de Groot was waiting for him at Susko Books, smoking a cigarette at the foot of the steps.

'More art catalogues, Rhonda?' Jack breathed the tobacco smoke in deeply as he went past and unlocked the front door. She dropped the butt and walked in behind him. No comment. The shop was still a mess. She paid no attention to that, either. Jack switched on the lights across the back wall but left the others off: the slightest glare was frying his eyeballs. He walked straight over to the counter, swung in behind it and picked up his bag, which was draped over the chair at his desk. He slung it over his shoulder.

'You know why I'm here,' she said.

Jack turned back to the buxom Rhonda de Groot. She was dressed all in white: a white short-sleeved shirt with a slightly military cut, white linen pants, and white low-heel sandals. Even a thick white bangle on her wrist. Everything tight over her proud roundness. She was still standing inside the front door. The door was closed behind her and she was holding a gun. Pointing it in Jack's general direction.

'The Sergius,' she said. She stepped towards Jack, just a metre or two, in case he could not see the gun properly. 'Thank you, Mr Susko.'

Jack put his hands up, about shoulder high. It was nearly 5.00 p.m. and his second gun for the day. Third since last Friday. There must have been a recent sale on small firearms somewhere. Next time, Jack might try to secure a little something for himself. Maybe a nice bazooka for under the counter.

'That's just lovely,' he said. 'But I don't have it. Okay?' As much as his entire head was a dull ache, Jack was all out of adrenaline: instead, a numb weariness flooded his body at the sight of Rhonda de Groot with a gun in her hand. 'Maybe you'd like to browse a little, see if another book might suit,' he said, motioning with his hand around the shop. 'Is it a present that you're looking for? Or something for yourself?'

Jack saw the red flash out of the barrel — like fire out

of a cartoon gun — before he heard the sound. The bullet ricocheted off something metallic behind him, maybe one of the steel beams in the concrete-block wall, and then embedded itself with a thud in a book somewhere. Jack wondered which title had been so severely dealt with.

'I don't have time, Mr Susko. Now.'

'You don't think anybody's going to hear that thing going off?'

She fired again. A pile of books on the counter that Kim had made earlier toppled over and collapsed to the floor. Jack looked down. This time, he could see the casualty: *What Food Is That? And How Healthy Is It?* by Jo Rogers. He might have to add a few dollars to its recommended retail price because of the free bullet in the spine.

'Look, Rhonda,' he said, calmly, though the second bullet had drained the remaining colour in his face and turned his feet into clumps of lead. 'This isn't going to get us anywhere. I don't have the Sergius. Who told you I did?'

Rhonda de Groot smiled. Unfortunately, it was not the kind of smile that made you feel better. 'Do you think the Sergius is something that could remain a secret?' she asked.

'Jesus. You sound like Kablunak.'

She lifted the gun higher, aimed it more towards his head. 'Viktor? When did you speak to him?'

'Earlier today. We went for a drive. It was great fun.'

'He's knows you've got the Bible?'

'He was the first, Rhonda. When did you find out?'

She became thoughtful. '*Shit*,' she said to herself, her body relinquishing its hard pose by just a fraction. 'So he's got it.'

Jack mulled over the idea: maybe it would get Rhonda

de Groot the hell out of his shop.

'Yeah,' he said. 'Vik's got the Sergius. It's all over.'

She did not like the news. She stiffened again, waved the black weapon in her hand and shifted her weight between her legs, as though getting ready to pop another cap off.

'How about you lower the gun?' said Jack, as nicely as he could.

The gun stayed where it was. Rhonda was frowning, thinking about something. 'Explain to me how Viktor got it.'

Whatever she was thinking about, Jack had no idea: and you should always know a little of what was going on to make a lie sound convincing. He lowered his arms, now felt his heart pounding his rib cage, like the fist-smack of a Las Vegas heavyweight on the big bag. Delayed reaction to bullets whizzing past him. Adrenaline motoring through his veins again. 'Do you mind if I sit down? I'm not as young as I used to feel.'

'Don't move.' Rhonda de Groot was a fan of the classics.

'Okay,' said Jack. He tried to read her face, but with only the one bank of lights on behind the counter, Susko Books was streaked with shadows. He tried to change the subject. 'I take it you're not here on behalf of your husband.'

She smiled. 'And what makes you say that?'

'He would have sent Lewis.'

'That would have been obvious.'

'But your gun's nice and subtle, huh?'

Rhonda lowered the piece a little, so that she did not have to speak over it. 'Don't think I won't use it.'

'You already have.'

'Tell me about Viktor.'

'It's only early days. We haven't been seeing each other long. But I'm not sure that I can trust him.'

'Just so you know, Mr Susko. I'm not one of those women who find funny men attractive.'

'That explains your husband.'

She managed a grin. 'No, Mr Susko. Explaining my husband would require a lifetime. Which I no longer have.'

Jack sensed a little marital disharmony. 'It wasn't nice of Richard, was it?' he said, sympathetically. 'Not telling you about the Sergius, using the gallery to hide it like that.'

'That's the least of his misdemeanours.' Her voice became deeper, lower, weighed down by whatever those misdemeanours were. For a moment they must have flashed through her mind and she narrowed her eyes as she replayed them. 'If only you knew, Mr Susko.'

'That why you want the Sergius? New life?'

She did not answer, shook a little, then shrugged: the last thoughts of her husband fell from Rhonda de Groot's blow-dried coiffure like dry, dead leaves. She straightened her shoulders. Gun up. Back to business.

'Sorry I can't help you,' said Jack.

She stood there, rigid, the air around her contracting as anger swelled in her bosom.

'Who told you I had the Sergius?'

'Your cousin, Mr Susko.'

'Oh good.' Jack rubbed his face in exasperation. 'Another name off the Christmas list.'

'Not a very clever lad.'

'On his father's side. Nothing to do with me.'

'He led us straight here the other night. We waited while he looked.' She swept the gun around the shop. 'Just a pity it wasn't here. I'd be in Paris now.'

'I was thinking Mexico myself.'

'What a shame.'

The door to Susko Books swung open. Rhonda half turned towards it, dropping the gun to her side at the same time. Somebody leaned into the shop, holding on to the door handle.

'Aren't you closed yet?' It was Tony Chan, from upstairs in the porn shop. He worked the afternoon shift while Deepak went home to sleep a couple of hours. He glanced at Rhonda but paid her no attention.

Jack nodded. 'Last sale of the day.'

'I'm off to the pub,' said Tony, almost breathlessly, as though he had been working his arse off. All Tony Chan did all day was stand behind the counter and watch DVDs; and even that from only one until six. 'Feel like a drink?'

'Feel like ten.'

'I can wait.'

Jack looked at Rhonda, then back at his neighbour. 'Won't be a minute.'

'Cool.' Tony held up a packet of cigarettes. 'I'll just be out here.'

He stepped out and closed the door behind him.

'Got to go, Rhonda.'

The gun came up again, stubby black barrel straight at Jack.

'Come on, Rhonda, you can't —'

The door to Susko Books swung open again, only this time with a rush. Lewis stood in the doorway. Jaw tight, eyes contracted, neck short and thick. He looked at Rhonda, rushed over and grabbed her by the arm.

'What the hell are you doing?' he said, almost hissing. 'Are you crazy?' He took the gun from her hand. 'I told you not to do anything stupid!'

'I couldn't wait any longer.'

'*Fuck* ...'

'Get your hands off me!'

Lewis shook her a little, continued to hold her by the arms. Rhonda grimaced, tried to struggle, but gave up soon enough.

She said: 'It's not here, Lew.'

The big man's attention shifted to Jack. He let go of Rhonda and took a couple of steps towards him. Lewis was wearing a tight red T-shirt with a black circle over the chest, like a giant ON button. Pair of navy-blue three-quarter-length shorts and leather hiking sandals. The skin on his arms and legs was taut and hairless and shiny, and everything beneath it twitched and flinched as he walked. He looked like an action figure come to life, all chest and narrow waist.

It was hardly a fair fight. But survival had its own rules. Jack wondered if he should eye-gouge or go a hard right foot to the guy's nuts. Or take Lewis and himself out simultaneously with a glorious, final head-butt.

'If you have it, you'd better tell me,' said Lewis, poking a thick, stubby forefinger into Jack's shoulder. His South African accent was as thick as his neck. Heat seemed to pulse off him, as though he was a truck engine after a fast run on the highway.

Jack shook his head. 'Not here ... *Lew.*'

'Let me tell you, Mr Susko. Bring that fucking Bible to me. Or I will hurt you.'

'He says Viktor's already got it,' said Rhonda behind him.

'Really?' Lewis laughed. 'What if I said I didn't believe you, Susko?'

Jack thought of Tony, outside having a cigarette. No use calling out: the part-time retail assistant at *Sydney's Largest Range of Adult Entertainment!* could give a lot of mouth but weighed not much more than a council newsletter.

Lewis continued to smile. He had the teeth equivalent of cauliflower ears. He leaned in and whispered. 'Don't make me hurt your girlfriend.'

'What?' Jack felt a little shock flash through him.

Rhonda de Groot frowned at the bodyguard. 'What girlfriend?'

'Larissa,' he said. 'I really should get back and give her some water. It has been a very hot day.'

Jack stared at the big guy, not quite believing him. 'Don't do anything stupid, Lewis.'

'That's for you to think about. She told me about the Sergius, Susko. Kablunak doesn't have it, does he? Because you're waiting for it in the mail.'

Behind him, Rhonda said: 'You son of a bitch!' Then to Lewis, firmly: 'What's Larissa got to do with this?'

He kept his back to her, turned his profile slightly and spoke over his shoulder. 'She's found God and wants her own special Bible.'

'Fucking little — !'

'Oh yes. And she's been talking to Mr Susko here. I followed her to his place. They talked all through the night. And even a little in the morning. Who knows what plans they have. Start a new Bible group, maybe?'

'I'm Hindu,' said Jack.

'I knew it!' snapped Rhonda. 'I told Richard she was no good.'

'What if I gave the Sergius to the cops? So nobody gets it?' Jack said it, but knew it was just talk. His mouth was the only place in his body that had not lost feeling.

'Oh, but somebody *would* get it, Susko. Your girlfriend. And *you*.'

'Does your boss know you're pulling a doozy on him?' asked Jack. He looked over at Rhonda. 'With the wife?'

Lewis smiled grimly. He held it for a while, then took a step back. He rolled his shoulders and cracked his neck with two sharp movements, left then right. He linked his arm through Rhonda's. 'Bible, Jack. I'll be waiting. Come to the gallery as soon as you have it. Or you may as well call an ambulance.'

Rhonda and Lewis walked out of Susko Books together. Tony Chan poked his head in through the door after them.

'Ready?'

Jack shook his head. 'Something's come up. Another time?'

'Sure. I'll be at the Edinburgh if you change your mind.'

'Have fun.'

Tony pointed a thumb over his shoulder. 'Jesus,' he said. 'That guy was a big motherfucker.'

'Yeah, he was.'

The door closed. Jack went over to the counter and leaned against it.

So. He looked around: the place was more than a little worse for wear. Just like its owner. The smell of gunshot drifted through the air. For the first time in a long time, Jack did not feel like hanging around. The truth of it threw him. Was it a premonition? A sign? Was he really going to lose Susko Books? And what the hell would he do if he did?

He killed the lights, locked the front door. He hoped Kim had something to drink. And plenty of painkillers.

~22~

IT WAS WELL AFTER 7.00 P.M. by the time Jack reached Surry Hills.

'You made it,' said Kim, as she opened the front door of the Crown Street terrace.

'Just.'

She looked at him closer. 'Oh my God! Are you okay?'

'Some aspirin would be lovely.'

'Come in, come in.'

Jack followed her down the hall. The house was cluttered but clean. There was a mountain bike against the wall, some cardboard boxes, and a wooden chair with a pot plant on the seat. Beside it, an old dressmaker's dummy, with pins stuck in it here and there like a giant voodoo doll.

'That Shane?'

She nodded. 'I glued his face on but it fell off with the humidity.'

At the end of the hall a shallow step led down into the kitchen, a 1960s relic, all laminex and linoleum and pastel-green cupboards. Kim pointed to a circular dining table.

'Take a seat. I think there's something in here.' She rummaged through a drawer.

'Got anything alcoholic?'

She turned, gave him a sympathetic look. 'I think Shane's got something in his room.'

'Tall glass,' he said. 'About a metre ought to do it.'

'Do you need a doctor?'

'Just a holiday. Want to come?'

Kim smiled. She had changed out of her earlier outfit: now she was wearing a red-and-blue-check Western shirt with pearl press-studs, and a black leather miniskirt, her slim legs smooth and endless below. Still the red Converse on her feet. She handed Jack a glass of water and a couple of tablets. 'Nurofen. Wait here.'

Kim went back out into the hallway. Jack heard her hollow footsteps up the stairs, and then floorboards creaking above his head. He wondered if it was a good idea to have come back to Kim's place. Did Kablunak's boys know her? Or Lewis? They probably all knew that Shane lived here, so there was always the chance someone might come over for a look. Maybe. Jack slumped in the chair, the day in his lap like a wet dog. From now on, he was swinging first. He washed down the tablets.

Kim came back holding up a bottle of Chivas Regal. 'What do you think?'

'I think you're very talented.'

She bowed with a flourish, then collected some glasses from a cupboard. She sat opposite Jack at the dining table.

'So what's the next move?' she asked, handing Jack a Scotch.

'Got any cigarettes?'

Kim reached for her bag hooked on the back of her chair, opened it and tossed him a crumpled packet. He shook for a cigarette. None came out. He inspected the soft-pack more closely, stuck his finger in it, then sighed. The gods really wanted him to stay off the darts.

'Is it empty?'

Jack nodded. Drank a good length of Scotch.

'Come on,' she said, eagerly. 'What are we going to do?'

'Why would you want to get involved?'

'Don't know. Nice eyes, maybe.'

For once, the flush to Jack's face was not the result of a blow to the body.

'I love your shirt, by the way.' She reached over and felt the printed cotton between her fingertips. There were small peacocks on it, pale rose and green and cream over blue. Plus a little blood now. It *was* a nice shirt, left over from when Jack used to have the odd dollar to spend.

'Beautiful fabric. Soft as a favourite handkerchief.'

'Just don't blow your nose on it.'

Her hand lingered a moment on Jack's sleeve. Her touch was soft, her fingers gentle, feeling the fabric as though it was telling her something. 'I've got some shirts that would look great on you,' she said, her voice lower, a trace of huskiness at the edges.

'Fashion designer?'

'That's me. Paris, London, New York. Bondi market stall.'

The Scotch was putting colour back into his cheeks. Kim was putting it everywhere else.

'The book Shane wanted you to pick up from me,' he said. 'Ever mention it before?'

Kim leaned back and crossed her arms and frowned. 'No. Has it got something to do with those guys?'

Jack brought the glass of Scotch to his lips, paused. 'It's their book.'

'I don't get it.'

'Shane stole it from them and now they want it back.'

'So how did you get it?'

'Shane sent it to me.'

'What?'

'It's complicated.'

'What kind of book is it?'

Jack stretched his neck carefully. 'The kind that attracts guns.'

'God.' Kim slumped her shoulders. She stared out into the back yard for a moment. 'So you've got the book that everybody wants?'

'Not exactly.'

'What do you mean?'

'More complications.' Jack sighed. He felt suddenly exhausted. 'It's still in the mail.'

'Didn't he just send me to pick it up?'

'Uh-huh.'

Kim was thinking. Her eyes held Jack's.

'I'm being punished in this life so that I may attain peace in the next,' he said.

She reached over and poured more Scotch into his glass. 'So the book's in the mail and they want you to give it to them as soon as it arrives? Or else?'

'Pretty much.'

'So just give it to them. Who cares about Shane?'

'Believe me, I'm not worried about Shane.' Jack delicately felt the back of his head. Blood was crusted in his hair. 'The problem is they're not the only *them* who want it.'

Kim grimaced on Jack's behalf. She leaned back, thoughtful. The chair creaked beneath her. After a moment, she angled her head slightly and gazed at Jack. 'How much is it worth?'

He picked up his glass, swirled it. 'Whims would not be a financial strain.'

'Well … why don't *you* keep it? Take the money and run?'

Jack grinned. 'It's an option. After today I've been giving it some thought.'

'And?'

'Too complicated. It's still a famous *stolen* antiquarian book, not actual money yet. And it's all too rushed. You need time to come up with a good plan. Contacts.' Jack remembered driving his old boss Ziggy Brandt around. His activities were often illegal, often complicated, but never rushed. And he was still out there, not rushing, which was probably proof enough of the formula.

'Maybe you just need some help?' Kim looked at Jack, helpfully. 'You need to jump on things when they come by.'

'What if you're on a moving train over a deep gorge?'

She shrugged. 'I just think that life is full of possibilities. And when they come … jump.'

Cicadas started up outside, the noise instantly loud and penetrating, as though they had dropped the clutches on a thousand two-stroke motorbikes, all at the same time. Jack looked out into the narrow yard through the glass-panelled doors to his left. Yeah. It sure would be great. Possibilities just falling in your lap. And the girl, too.

Kim screwed the cap off the Scotch and poured Jack some more. 'So when do you think this book is going to arrive?'

'It already has.'

'What?'

'At the post office. They delivered the pick-up slip the other day.'

'Hang on. So you could just go and get it?'

Jack nodded. 'Yep.'

'So … ?'

He saw the look in her eyes, could read the excitement, the sparks of possibility that her imagination flicked up like flint being struck. He recognised it. The impulse was his own. 'They've been through my apartment, they've been through my shop. If I'd have picked it up, it would be gone by now,' he said. 'But while it's there, I've got a bargaining chip. So the post office is the safest place for it at the moment. Nobody knows it's there.'

'But if they knew, could they pick it up?'

'I don't think so, not without the slip.'

'Is it registered? Do you need a signature?'

'No, but without the slip, they'd still need ID. They'd need to be me.'

'Or get a very slack postal worker.'

Jack shrugged.

'Always the chance,' said Kim.

'Still safer than my place. And anyway, they don't know it's there. And even if they did, the post office doesn't open again until 9.00 a.m. tomorrow, so I've got some time up my sleeve.'

'To do what?'

'I'm still thinking.'

'You look like you're in pain. Maybe you should lie down.'

'I'd hate to be rude.'

She gazed into her Scotch, swirled the glass. 'Why not? It wouldn't bother me.'

Jack looked at Kim Archer. He said nothing and kept looking. She did not seem to mind.

'It wouldn't bother me, either,' he said and finished his drink.

~23~

THERE WAS A KNOCK ON THE FRONT DOOR. Jack rolled onto his back, his sleep only lightly dented by the sound, like a teaspoon tap on a soft-boiled egg; then just as he was about to slip under again, another knock. He could feel clammy skin pressed against him down his left side. Jack remembered whose clammy skin it was and thought about turning over and putting an arm around it. But the room was too hot, still and heavy with stale air, and Jack needed a drink. He tried to swallow, but his mouth was full of rust. The thought of a glass of water stirred his dehydrated brain some more. A third knock at the front door finally did the trick and Jack opened his eyes.

The room was pitch black: there were no dimensions to

it and he felt a little dizzy. He looked for something to hold
on to with his eyes. After a moment, he could just make out
the curtained window, a square of pale night flat against the
wall across from the foot of Kim's bed. With an anchor laid,
Jack strained his ears into the darkness, listening.

This time the knock was louder. Kim shifted beside him.
Who the hell was there? It was the middle of the night.
Better if he went and checked in case there was some kind
of trouble — because if there was, Jack figured he was
probably responsible for bringing it over.

He got out of bed and felt around on the floor for his
jeans. After the blow to his head and the Chivas Regal, it was
more difficult than it should have been. Got his jeans on,
finally. He walked unsteadily down the stairs and along the
hall, his bare feet sucking at the polished floorboards with
every step. He paused before the front door. 'Who is it?' he
said, in a loud, annoyed whisper.

'It's me,' said a surprised voice. 'Who's that?'

Jack swore. He swung the door open. 'How's it going,
Carl?'

Carl stared, did not answer. Then he walked in, straight
past Jack and down the hall. He knew where he was going.

They went into the kitchen. Jack poured a glass of water
and drank it and then poured another and drank that, too.
He sat down at the dining table. Carl stood. It was just after
5.30 a.m. There was the nearly empty bottle of Scotch left
on the dining table. And the cousins, Jack and Carl. Under
the weak kitchen light, with the lino and the laminex and
the pale pastels around them, it was as though they had gone
back in time: a bottle of brandy instead of the Scotch, and
they could have been in Aunt Eva's kitchen, so many years

ago. Though Jack had not admitted it to himself at the time, when he met Renée at the house in Bankstown, he had felt the urge to step inside and look around, see the old rooms from his childhood weekends: hiding places in the bedroom closets, and the see-through plastic runner down the hall that you could slide over with a run-up. He remembered one particular Sunday, church-day afternoon, in the kitchen at Aunt Eva's house in Bankstown. Full of people milling around, eating and drinking. Carl with his Messerschmitt, dive-bombing the walnut cakes and shortbreads on the table. And Jack's aunt talking to somebody about her deceased husband. 'Oh, yes, he loved confession,' she was saying. 'He used to go in regularly and confess to things he hadn't done yet. He called it *building up credit*.' Her tone was bitter. 'Then he'd go out and get up to all sorts of no good.' An old woman shook her head and made the sign of the cross, though Jack remembered thinking it was not a bad idea.

'I thought Shane might be here,' said Carl, his tone all tough-guy-taking-no-shit.

'At five-thirty in the morning? You must be good friends.'

'Yeah. So what?'

'He's not here.'

'But you are.'

'Looks like it.'

Carl nodded. Then stuck his chin out a little and pouted.

'I hear you're pretty good at the Palomino,' said Jack. 'That your *Rebel without a Cause* routine?'

'Fuck off.' Carl slid his hands into the tight pockets of his jeans. Looked around the kitchen. 'I'm not doing anything.'

Jack saw Kim's mobile lying on the dining table.

'Okay,' he said, reaching for it. He flipped the phone open. 'I promised Renée I'd call her when I saw you again. She's been worried.'

'What?' Carl's cool demeanour went up like a struck match. 'Hey, no ...'

'Excuse me?'

'Don't call her.'

'Why not?' said Jack, contemplating the Chivas because his head was pounding and his eyes felt like little bags of hot sand. 'I like Renée,' he said. 'And I don't like you.'

Carl closed his eyes for a second. Opened them again. 'Please,' he said.

Jack looked at him for a moment. He closed the mobile and put it down on the dining table. 'Better start from the beginning.'

'You've got to help me, Jack.' Carl held his hands up in a gesture of sincerity. 'I'm in big trouble.'

Jack said nothing.

'Did you hear me?'

'Yeah, I heard you.' Jack's voice was low but firm. He felt the blood flow into his hands and pulse at the back of his head. 'How about you give me the keys back,' he said, holding out his hand. 'Or did you drop them at Susko Books while you trashed the place?'

Carl stared down at the floor, shook his head seriously. 'No, no, no,' he said, then looked back up at Jack. 'That was *not* me. I let 'em in, but that was not me.'

'You let them in, but it wasn't you?' Jack swore. 'My shop's all over the floor and you're telling me it's got nothing to do with you? And what about the damage to my apartment?'

'I told you, I had to let them in! They've got me by the

balls, Jack. You've got to understand.'

Jack picked up the bottle of Chivas Regal and turned it in his hand. 'All right, Carl. Let's do it then. Who, what and why. From the beginning.'

'Have you got a cigarette?'

'No.'

Carl ran a hand through his hair. 'Richard de Groot,' he announced. 'He wants the Sergius back. And if I don't get it to him, I'm cactus.'

'That's it?'

Carl nodded.

'Richard de Groot busted my place up?'

'Yeah. Well, mainly Lewis.'

'And you let them in?'

'That's right.'

Jack shook his head in disbelief. 'You found the spare keys to Susko Books in the car and then rang de Groot and said *Hey, I've got the keys, come round and have a look for your Bible?*'

'No.' Carl took a breath, looked away. 'Not like that. They caught me in your shop the first time. Lewis was staking the place out, saw me going in. *Then* they made me go to your apartment.'

'So *you* were looking for the Sergius at Susko Books, not de Groot? How the fuck did you know about it?'

Carl paused for a moment. 'Larissa.'

'Christ.' Jack picked up the Chivas bottle and poured a couple of fingers' worth in the glass he had been drinking from last night. He drank. The Scotch let go its fire and reamed his throat with heat. 'Larissa told you to go see if the Sergius was at Susko Books?

'That's right.'

Jack thought about it. She was checking to see if he had lied about it not turning up. Okay. Nature of the business. No need to get too upset. 'So you and Larissa, huh?'

'It's not what you think.'

'That's a very tired line, cousin.'

'Yeah, well it's true.' Carl tried to look insulted but maybe should have practised more. 'We're just good friends.'

'I don't even want to know.'

'We *talk*. All right with you?'

'You sure it's me you've got to ask?'

Carl put his hands on his hips, went to say something, but kept it down.

Jack let it go: he could feel other questions start to prickle his scalp, like spiders' legs hustling around his head. It was not a pleasant sensation. 'Why was Lewis staking Susko Books out?'

'I don't know. Waiting for the Sergius, I suppose.'

'Right.' Jack tried to sift the facts. The dubious ones floated to the surface like old champagne corks. Why would de Groot think that he had the Sergius?

'Jack. I need that fucking Bible.'

'Or what?'

Carl stood a little taller, puffed out his chest. 'I'm fucking serious.'

Jack's hackles hackled. He squeezed the bottle of blended malt and then shook it. He placed the bottle back down, slowly and precisely. He wished he had a cigarette in his hand so that he had something else to think about other than curling it up into a fist. 'You said you came here looking for Shane,' he said. 'What for?'

Carl took a moment. 'Help.'

'How?'

'I don't know! De Groot's going to stick Lewis onto me for fuck's sake! Rearrange my face if I don't bring him the fucking Bible. I'm running around like crazy trying to get out of this mess and my wife's kicked me out and there's no money for the bills and shit and … and … *fuck*.'

'You came round on the Friday night,' said Jack, remembering, holding Carl in his sights. 'Right after the De Groot Galleries heist. You knew about it all along.'

'Yeah, I knew it was going down. I went around to watch.'

'What for?'

'Opportunities. What else?'

'Like what?'

Carl shrugged. 'Like … something. I don't know,' he said.

'Jesus,' said Jack. 'I didn't realise I was related to a criminal genius.'

Carl curled his top lip into a snarl. 'Didn't you use to work for Ziggy Brandt?'

'I work for myself. Who do you work for?'

'My family.'

'And doing a fine job, too.'

Jack thought he might have pushed it too far, but Carl flushed and shifted his eyes away. 'All right. I've fucked up. But now you've got to help me, Jack.'

'That night you came over and borrowed the car. Why?'

'I needed it, simple as that. I saw you come out of the gallery and couldn't fucking believe it. And the Toyota when you drove off … Like Mum was driving it. I almost yelled out.' He paused. 'Still don't know why she gave it to you.' There was bitterness in his voice.

'Keep the fucking thing.'

Carl stared blankly at his cousin. 'Can I have a drink? Please?'

'The tap is right behind you.'

'That's it?'

'More stories, Carl.' Jack shifted in his chair. 'And be aware that I'm currently in the throes of nicotine withdrawal.'

A pause. 'You here with Kim?'

Jack saw his cousin's brow tighten slightly over his eyes. 'None of your concern,' he said, tone hard as ice. He slugged more Scotch. His head felt a little better, if not his predicament. 'So Larissa's had you in from the beginning. Keeping an eye on Shane, I suppose.' Jack held the glass of Chivas up, closed an eye and aimed it at the ceiling light. 'But Shane's not here and neither is the Sergius. De Groot's after you and the wife's changed the locks. Looks like you're pretty shit at everything, cousin.'

'You got a big mouth.' The fridge started to hum. Carl glanced at it, put a hand on his slim hip, dragged the other one through his hair and tried to look mean.

'That meant to be scary? What else you got?'

'Fuck off.'

'Not the way it's going to work,' said Jack. He kicked the chair opposite and stretched out his legs. 'Did Larissa tell you about the Sergius job?'

Carl sensed the growing violence in Jack's mood. He sat down, slumped forward with his elbows on the table, tiredness like a wet coat over his shoulders. 'Look, I can't even fucking remember anymore. I overheard Shane and Walter talking about the job at one of our shows. When I told Larissa, I think she already knew about it.'

'You're all in that theatre group?'

'Yeah, the Palomino. Just down the road, on Devonshire.'

'With Walter. Who's with the Russian?'

'Yeah. Good actor. Really fat. He got Shane a job once before. I heard them talking about this new job at a rehearsal a couple of weeks ago. Shane asking Walter if he could swing any more work his way. Said he really needed the cash. He kind of invited himself along, though from what I could tell Kablunak needed an extra.'

'And you teamed up with Larissa.'

'Jack, I *really* need the money. The building industry has slowed right down. I'm lucky if I get a job changing a fucking light globe.'

Jack nodded but had stopped listening. He was working it out — and the view was all clear around Larissa Tate. The girl could juggle half-a-dozen buzzing chainsaws and never get a scratch. She worked for de Groot and knew all about the Sergius. Then Shane told her all about his new heist job and *presto*, she's got her inside man. Then knucklehead Carl comes along and she works out a way to use him, too. Jack just lands conveniently in her lap, thanks to Australia Post. Cheap insurance on every bet, any way you look at it.

'How does Richard de Groot come in connected to you?' asked Jack.

'I told you. Lewis busted me going into Susko Books.'

'Yeah, fine. But what was Lewis doing there to begin with?'

Carl dropped his head. He looked like a tired, stressed electrician father of three with a broken van and a lonely wife. 'I called de Groot earlier. Offered him the Sergius. He must have sent Lewis to keep an eye on me.'

Jack grinned. 'You thought you'd go it alone.'

'I don't owe Larissa a fucking thing. I got a family, Jack.'

'What did de Groot say?'

'Ten thousand.'

Jack thought back to his own offer from Richard de Groot, after the heist.

'What was I going to do with a hundred grand's worth of Bible?' said Carl, holding out his hands. 'Sell it at a fucking church stall on a Sunday afternoon?'

So Carl did not know about the three-point-four. Jack wondered if he should tell him.

'I thought I could sell it back to de Groot, you know?' continued Carl. 'I figured that'd be the easiest way to make quick cash.' He drummed the table with his fingers. 'And I'd heard stories. I wasn't going to fuck around with the Russian.'

'So you offered it to de Groot, but you didn't have possession of it?'

'Larissa told me some shit about Shane lying low for a while and that we'd sort everything out in a few days. I didn't believe her. Then I followed her to your place. You were there when the job went down on the Friday, and now Larissa was popping in for a chat.' He looked accusingly at Jack. 'And she stayed all night, too.'

'So I'm in with Larissa, huh?'

'Why not? You used to work for Ziggy Brandt. Why wouldn't you be?' He nodded. 'Opportunity knocks.'

'Of course. And obviously the Sergius was with me.'

'Correct.' Carl's eyes narrowed a little as he looked at Jack. 'I didn't think it'd be a problem to get hold of it.' He tapped his pocket. 'Seeing as I had the spare keys.'

Jack picked up the bottle of Scotch. He splashed a little into Kim's glass and pushed it over to his cousin, and then poured the rest for himself. Drank. 'I don't have it,' he said.

Carl closed his eyes for a moment, controlled himself. 'Do you have to be such an arsehole? Jesus Christ.'

Jack drank some more Scotch. 'Carl. I don't have it.'

'You've got to give de Groot the Bible.' Carl's voice cracked a little: it was a sinner's voice, thick with remorse and regret. 'I can't let Renée find out about any of this. She'd never take me back. Not this time.'

'De Groot's not going to give you any money, Carl, believe me. You should just go home and forget about it.'

'Yeah, sure. After Lewis breaks my legs, I'll just crawl down Old Canterbury Road.'

A little sympathy welled somewhere inside Jack. He tried to weigh his cousin's sincerity, but it was too early in the morning for a clear reading. 'I can't give you the Bible.'

Carl turned away in disgust.

'Look. Kablunak wants it, and there are my own legs to consider. And, just so you know, Lewis wants it, too. He's in with de Groot's wife. And Richard is not included.'

'What?'

'You heard. And they've got Larissa somewhere. Either I give them the Sergius or else.'

Carl frowned, digesting everything Jack was saying. None of it was going to help him.

'So everybody wants the fucking thing,' continued Jack. 'And I'm the goddamn lamb shank in the stew. Not you.'

A phone started ringing. Carl reached into his pocket and pulled out his mobile. He looked at the screen. 'Fuck.' He hit the phone against his leg and swore some more, his face pale, his eyes red and flitting. 'Fucking de Groot.'

'You'd better answer it.'

'And what am I going to say?'

Jack looked down at his glass of Scotch. Two rings later, he said: 'Tell him I want to talk to him.'

Carl stared at Jack, stunned. 'Yeah?'

Jack nodded, held up his hand for the phone. Carl blew a hard breath and answered the call. 'Yeah, it's me … Yep … Yeah, I've found him … Yeah, but listen … He wants to talk to you … Okay? … Hang on …'

Jack stood up. Carl handed him the mobile.

'Richard,' he said. 'How's my favourite four-foot art thief doing?'

~24~

IT WAS GETTING ON FOR 6.30 A.M. NOW. A police van screamed
by as Jack turned the Fiori right onto Oxford Street. As early
as it was, there was already traffic around: a selection of cars
and cabs, delivery trucks, buses and the odd moped. There
were people walking the footpaths. It was a hot, restless,
almost-lit morning, the half-hidden moon backlighting
the late dark with a smoky pearl haze. The sky was busy,
gathering storm clouds to itself, like a shearer pulling in
folds of wool. Soon, the rush of rain would come. Relief.

Maybe.

Jack was in no hurry to get to Richard de Groot's house
in Vaucluse. He was tired, sore, and felt on the outside of
everything that had happened over the last few days, even

though on paper he looked to be right in the middle of it. De Groot had been cocky on the phone, all laughs and *sure, Jack, no worries*, exuding enough *smug* to pollute a small city. They did not talk long, but Jack made it sound like he was selling and de Groot made it sound like he was buying — though Jack was surprised when de Groot insisted he come over right away.

'I've got plenty of time right now,' he said. 'Plenty of cash, too.'

'And why wait for our Russian friend?'

De Groot hesitated. 'Yes.' Then: 'Shall we get it over with?'

'Why not?'

'Good. We'll share a couple of champagne cocktails and watch the storm come in.'

'What's the address?'

The South African told him. 'And Jack,' he had added. 'Just you. No cousin, okay? He irritates me.'

'Fine. Keep your thug out of it as well.'

De Groot laughed. 'Don't keep me waiting.'

Jack parked the car. He reached across and locked the passenger side door, glancing down at his bag beside him on the seat. Any key could open Chester's Fiori, but Jack doubted it was the kind of vehicle car thieves sought out in this suburb. And better not to have the bag with him when he spoke with de Groot. He shoved it under the seat.

De Groot's place was on the upside of Vaucluse Road, a huge, modern-style house of grey stone tiles and long, sheer tinted windows, flush with the tile-work so that in the pale-moonlit morning every wall looked as smooth as a sheet of metal.

Three storeys and some kind of rooftop deck area, too, all set behind a high wall of the same grey stonework as the house, and a shiny steel gate that stretched across a curved, concrete driveway leading down to underground parking. Minimalist, architect-designed, probably around five or six mill. Or maybe ten or eleven: what the hell did Jack know? All he was sure about was the going rate on rare, fourteenth-century illuminated Bibles.

He surveyed the scene, a little nervous now. It was a nice stretch of real estate. With the city shimmering in the distance and plenty of Sydney Harbour in front of it and the light-topped masts on the big yachts gently swaying on the glimmer of water, just down the hill: you could always see where you parked your boat. And even with the sky getting a little apocalyptic, there was still something to look at and feel good about looking at.

There was a shuddering noise. Jack saw the long steel gate of the de Groot residence sliding open. He could hear the echo of an engine being revved from down below. Hard and loud. Just before the gate reached the end of its track, there was an almighty squeal of tyres, and a deep roar of acceleration and within seconds the nose of a car was at the top of the driveway.

The de Groot Maserati. It edged out onto the road, its front grille like the snout of a pissed-off guard dog, with someone tugging hard at the leash around its neck. The windows were tinted, and in the sombre light Jack could not see the driver. Richard de Groot? Surely not.

The car sped off, back in the direction of the city. Why

would de Groot go now? Leave Jack and three-and-a-bit million behind?

Jack stared down the road, where the car had already disappeared. *No. He wouldn't.*

~25~

Jack pressed the buzzer set beneath an eyeball video camera on the left of the barred front gate. No answer. Through the bars he could see a brick-paved path that swung away to the left. He could hear something bubbling, too: no doubt some kind of water feature. He buzzed again, looking into the lens as though he might see somebody at the other end. No answer again.

More thunder. Jack walked down to the garage entrance. It had not closed after the Maserati zoomed off. He looked at a couple of the neighbours' houses. Only their security lights showed. All was quiet and empty along Vaucluse Road. Jack felt like a loud noise as he walked down the curved concrete driveway and slipped in under the house.

No cars, but enough room to park four or five. No shelves, boxes or benches, either, no usual garage crap pushed up against the walls: just a spotless, well-lit rectangle that could have been leased out as a showroom floor. Two cream-painted doors at the rear wall. Jack chose the right. Behind it, leading up into the house, wide, black-veined white marble stairs. He started to climb. He called out: 'De Groot?' The house threw silence back at him.

At the top of the stairs, a long, cool hallway: Persian-style runner over more tiled floor, a couple of pieces of brushed steel and glass furniture, some artwork over the white walls.

'Hello? Anybody here?'

Jack listened. Still nothing. He wondered what he would say to the cops.

Cautiously down the hall, glancing at the stuff on display: a series of half-a-dozen watercolours, about forty centimetres square and box framed in blonde wood. Interesting subject matter — plucked chickens and roasted chickens and headless chickens and chickens on fire and gutted chickens hanging from hooks. Jack could not figure out if the de Groots liked chickens or if they were maybe vegetarians making a political statement. Probably just *de rigueur*. It reminded him of Kablunak eating in his office with his sleeves rolled up.

After all the poultry, a large, airy, cream-carpeted lounge room with high ceilings and lots of mirrors; on the Vaucluse Road side, a complete wall of double-glazed glass, the better to take in the harbour. Placed precisely around the room, sleek white-leather couches, beige shagpile rugs, ultra-modern lamps and chairs, and a couple of glass-top tables with nothing on them. A large Aboriginal dot painting was the featured artwork, taking up almost the entire right-hand-side wall, warm and luminous under subtle, professionally set-up lighting. Ancient Greek-style columns framed two doorways out of the room. The place was like a cross between a Mediterranean villa and a hotel lobby. The couches and seats looked ironed, the shagpile combed. Jack wondered if anybody had ever breathed in the place, let alone sat on anything.

He took the second doorway out of the lounge room. Another hall, not as grand as the first, but carpeted and quiet. An air-conditioning panel indicated a pleasant twenty-two degrees Celsius on its digital display.

Two more doors open on the right. Jack looked into a couple of large bedrooms, empty and so neat and unslept in they could have been mock-ups for a furniture catalogue shoot. At the end of the hallway, he turned right. First door, another neat white room with a great view out over the harbour. Somebody's study: large, modern executive desk; black leather executive chair; bookshelves; another smaller, ergonomic desk in the corner with a computer set up on it; a couple of oil paintings on the walls; and a vase on a stand with flowers blooming out of it.

Jack stepped inside. The flowers were arum lilies: hard to get in Sydney but kind of appropriate in their funereal way. Especially considering there was a dead body in the room.

~26~

RICHARD DE GROOT WAS LYING FACE-DOWN on the floor behind his desk. He was wearing a white bathrobe. It looked expensive and very comfortable. Jack guessed that de Groot would never have imagined when he bought it that he might die in it. But there you go. Death took no notice of high-quality, one hundred percent Egyptian cotton bathrobes. All comfort was fleeting. At least until the last lie-down.

Jack stepped closer. The black leather executive chair was pushed aside. De Groot's head was slumped inside the cavity of an open floor-safe, as though he was down on the ground after a hot trail hike, taking a long drink from a cold mountain stream. He had been shot in the back. Maybe while he was getting out a little money for Jack, to reward him for the Sergius.

Two gunshot wounds, right behind the heart. *Bang, bang.*

Jack knelt down and looked past de Groot's head. It was not a particularly large safe, maybe thirty centimetres long, twenty wide, and no more than a foot deep. It was empty. But a small fortune would have had no trouble being comfortable in there. Jack moved closer, the light hit a different angle and he saw that it was actually deeper than he had first thought: it also stretched further out left and right under the floor. *Jesus.* One hundred thousand gone? Two? More?

Jack stood up and something beside the desk caught his eye: it was a wad of money. Hundred-dollar notes. The word *fingerprints* flashed through his mind but had no visible effect on him. Jack reached over and picked up the money and moved away from Richard de Groot's body. Crisp bills packed tight, about two centimetres thick. The kind of thing Jack had always dreamed about having under his mattress.

Ten thousand dollars? Thereabouts. Two little centimetres of money. The killer had missed it. Among a lot of identical wads, it was easily missed.

'Keep it, Mr Susko.'

The blood in Jack's head drained out in one smooth, quick rush. For a second the picture before his eyes faltered and he felt a cold wave down his back. He turned towards the voice, almost dropping the money in his hands.

Viktor Kablunak stood in the doorway of de Groot's study. Behind him was Pascal, his arms crossed and chin high.

'Go on, keep it,' repeated Kablunak, nonchalant and generous, as though he was in his own home. 'Money is for the living.'

Jack lowered his arms. His thumb flicked at a corner of the small pad of cash, nervously. 'You killed him,' he said.

Kablunak laughed, looked behind him at Pascal, and then turned back to Jack. 'And why would I do that, Mr Susko?'

'For the Sergius.'

The Russian shook his head, looking like a teacher disappointed with a promising student. 'But you are holding the Sergius for me, Mr Susko. No? Why would I kill him for something that he does not have?'

Jack stood up straighter as the blood slowly returned to his head. Now it began to throb.

'There is nothing that Richard de Groot has that I would want,' said Kablunak. 'And would I wait for somebody to arrive?' He waved his hand, dismissing the whole notion, and stepped into the room. 'It is obvious somebody else killed him.'

'So what are you doing here?'

'Following you, Mr Susko.' Viktor Kablunak raised his eyebrows and nodded at the cash in Jack's hand. 'Making sure you don't do anything ... stupid.' He smiled. 'But go on. Keep the money. It is yours. A little bonus.'

Jack looked down at the wad in his hand. He tossed it onto the desk. 'I'll be right, thanks.'

'No, no, no,' said Kablunak. 'I insist. You *must*.'

'Why don't you have it?'

The Russian grinned. 'I have already wiped my arse today.'

'Remind me to use the bathroom at your place.'

'That is funny, Jack. Yes.' Kablunak walked over to the desk and picked up the money. He fanned a corner beneath his thick, manicured thumb. Then he held the cash out to

Jack. 'Nobody has seen this,' he said. 'It is free. Easy. Take it.'

'It's not mine.'

'Ah! I do not believe you, Mr Susko. Did Pascal hit you too hard?' The Russian scoffed. 'It is only money. It has no soul and cannot assume the soul of he who has it in his wallet. Listen to me. Money cannot be *possessed*. Money can only be *exercised*.' He nodded his head, smiled, and slapped the wad lightly against his leg. 'I like you. Let me tell you a secret and then maybe you will take this money and go and make your fortune and not ever again kneel before another man.' He walked past the desk to the window and gazed at the sky view, splintered with still-burning lights and strobed by the odd flash of lightning in the distance. 'Money is *energy*, Mr Susko,' he said. 'It is *electricity*. It *moves*. Its only purpose is to move. And it is attracted to those who help move it.' Kablunak turned and looked hard at Jack, his dark eyes glinting. 'Think, Mr Susko. Who wires their house with wood?' He held out the money again.

There was a murdered man lying on the floor beside Jack. He glanced down at de Groot's body again. It had been a long day and a long night. Looked like it was going to be a long morning, too.

'Take it,' said Kablunak again, his tone harder by a couple more notches. 'Take it. Or I will make you eat it.'

There was nothing to think about. Jack reached out, took the money from the Russian, and shoved it into the front pocket of his jeans.

There it was. Done. Depending on what happened in the end, Jack supposed he could always use it for bail money.

'Good. Very good.' Kablunak smiled, broadly. He walked

casually around the desk and stood next to Jack and looked down at de Groot's body. He slipped his hands into the pockets of his grey suit pants. 'So. Who?'

'I don't know.' Jack could smell Kablunak's aftershave and the intimacy added to his discomfort.

'Yes.' The Russian reached up to his face and felt the smoothness of his chin with his fingertips. 'Well.'

Jack nodded at de Groot's body. 'Your old friend.'

'Once upon a time.'

'What happened?'

Viktor Kablunak turned to Jack, stared at him a moment, expressionless, and then resumed looking down at de Groot's body on the floor. He said: 'The student surpasses the teacher.'

Jack felt the money in his pocket press against his leg. 'I didn't know you were Buddhist.'

Kablunak grinned. 'No, Mr Susko. My mother would be very upset at the mere mention. But perhaps our friend here will come back as a cockroach? I certainly hope so.'

'He might live longer that way.'

The Russian's face was serious, slightly pained. 'Yes.' He nudged de Groot's body with his shoe. 'Take note, Mr Susko. A man dead. And why? Because his judgement was clouded by his ego. He wanted to send me a message. Prove a point, as they say. Well, here is his reward.' Kablunak walked back towards the door, stopped and turned back to face Jack. 'The ego is a whorehouse, Mr Susko. But remember, there you fuck nobody but yourself.' He pointed a finger. 'You will come with me, now.'

Kablunak nodded at Pascal, who stepped into the room. He went over and stood by Jack.

'Let's go.'

Jack felt his adrenal glands start to pump. 'I'm not going anywhere.'

'Mr Susko.' Kablunak was in a crisp gun-metal-grey suit, even at this hour, with a deep-maroon shirt unbuttoned down his chest: but weariness was starting to show in his voice. 'I do not intend to let you out of my sight until the mail arrives later today. And you should hope that it is today.'

'What about de Groot? You just going to leave him here?'

'There is little I can do for him. His comfort is now in, or not in, depending on who you believe, the hands of God.' Viktor Kablunak made a quick, small sign of the cross. It was not particularly reverent. 'Such is the cycle and mystery of life.'

Pascal grabbed Jack by the arm.

'Wait.'

Kablunak looked sternly at Jack. 'I am not a morning person, Mr Susko.'

'I can't give you the Sergius.'

'Maybe you do not understand me. I am very *not pleasant* in the early morning.'

'I think I know who killed de Groot,' said Jack. 'Rhonda came to see me yesterday. With a gun. She wants the Sergius, too.'

'Rhonda?' Kablunak frowned.

'And Lewis,' added Jack, feeling sweat run down his spine. It was hot in the study and the air was heavy with heat and death and he did not want to be there anymore. 'If I don't get them the Bible, Lewis is going to pay me a visit. And they've got de Groot's assistant, Larissa Tate, and things aren't looking too healthy for her, either.' Jack wanted to take a deep breath but was going to wait until he got outside into the pre-storm air. 'I don't want blood on my hands, Viktor. Mine or anybody else's.'

'Lewis?' Pascal bristled like a dog with a rabbit scent in his nostrils. He turned to his boss. 'That motherfucker's here?'

'Apparently,' murmured Kablunak.

'So you see the predicament,' said Jack.

'Only yours, Mr Susko.' The Russian stared down at the body of Richard de Groot.

'How'd that prick Lewis get into the country?' asked Pascal, still holding on to Jack's arm.

Viktor Kablunak shrugged.

'Why would he have trouble getting into the country?' asked Jack.

'Because in South Africa he is a very bad man,' said Kablunak. He rubbed the back of his neck.

'Maybe you guys should start a club.'

'Do not think it is funny, Mr Susko. If Lewis has your girlfriend ...' The Russian waved his hand in the air. 'Well ... it is not good for her. A pity you cannot help.'

'She's not my girlfriend, Viktor. But it can't be like that.'

'You are in no position to say.'

The Russian's words were like a slap. And the truth of them was bitter and Jack could taste it now, like some foul liqueur burning down his throat. For him, there was going to be no Sergius, no lump sums, no deals no chances no happy endings. No goddamn land of the plenty. It was just going to be this dead man on the floor in front of him and whatever else he was about to step in next.

'See what it is to be powerless, Mr Susko?' Viktor

Kablunak eased a smooth smile across his lips.

'I'm only human, Viktor.'

'Well, Mr Susko, there is your problem. *Attitude.* Our limits are merely what we choose to accept.'

'Really? You saying I could play piano like Red Garland, if I wanted to?'

'I'm sure you have never even tried.'

'Why would I?'

'See what I mean, Mr Susko?'

'Okay. Right.' There was only one choice left open to him and Jack knew he was going to have to take it. So he looked the Russian in the eye and took it. 'You could help me,' he said.

Kablunak seemed to savour the request for a moment. 'And why should I do that, Mr Susko?'

'Crash those limits, Viktor. Try a little tenderness.'

The Russian laughed. 'You know, Mr Susko, I do like you.'

'So?'

'I would not advise that you bet on a shitty pair of sevens.'

Kablunak was right, but Jack had bet on less in the past and lived to tell Lois the tale. 'What's the time now?'

The Russian glanced at his watch. 'It is a quarter past seven.'

'I can have the Sergius in your hands in one hour and forty-five minutes.'

'Really?'

'Guaranteed.'

'Well. Good.' Viktor Kablunak nodded, slowly. Smiled a little more. 'So we are finally getting somewhere.'

'Where is it?' asked Pascal, looking confused.

Jack ignored him, stared at Kablunak. 'Well? Will you help me?'

'You were at pains yesterday, Mr Susko, to explain to me that the Sergius had not yet arrived.'

Jack shrugged. 'What can I say? When I go in to bat, it's usually for me.'

'Do not lie to me again,' said Kablunak. 'I do not own a dog, but I like to exercise my vengeance, Mr Susko. Regularly.'

'Okay.'

Pascal was up on the balls of his feet. 'What do you want to do?'

The Russian sighed, shook his head. 'There will be a storm and it will rain all day today. In truth, I want to go home and put my feet up and watch a good movie. Something like … *A Place in the Sun*.'

'I can bring popcorn,' said Jack.

'Do you like Elizabeth Taylor, Mr Susko?'

'Even in *Cleopatra*.'

'Yes. Well …' Kablunak checked his watch again. 'Let us hope that you do not get the same scathing reviews for your next performance.' He pulled at the cuffs of his shirt. 'And so. Where are we to witness the final scenes, Mr Susko?'

'Lewis wants me to go round to De Groot Galleries as soon as I have the Sergius.'

'Then that is where we shall go.'

'Now?'

'Of course.'

'How do you know he's going to be there?'

'Because I know lots of things, Mr Susko.'

'Yeah? What number am I thinking of now?'

'Three-point-four million,' said Kablunak, face in the ballpark of *deadpan* to *not impressed*. 'Minus expenses. And I would advise you to keep out of that column in my ledger. Mr Susko.'

~27~

THE CITY HUMMED ACROSS THE WATER like a giant oil rig, coloured lights winking over the harbour. Pascal walked Jack a short distance down Vaucluse Road to the Fiori for his bag, and then walked him back to the Mercedes parked out in front of de Groot's house. Walter was sitting behind the wheel, staring out of the side window at the view. Viktor Kablunak was in the front seat beside him, eyes closed and head back on the leather upholstery, like a weary passenger on a long-haul flight. Above them, there were lights left on inside the de Groot residence. Jack was having trouble shaking Richard de Groot's bathrobed body from his mind, on the floor of the study like that, head hanging in the empty safe, bloodied and dead. He was glad a couple of the lights had been left burning with their hot, halogen brightness. He was not a religious man, but around death there was always that inclination. Jack remembered Aunt Eva talking about how she had sat with her husband all through the night when he passed away. So that his earthly body was safe while the ghost road was taken. Even though she could not stand him, regularly, in life. Jack found himself grateful for the light up in those windows.

Pascal reached across him and opened the rear door of the Merc.

'You guys do this often?' asked Jack.

'What's that?'

'Leave bodies behind to fend for themselves?'

'You want to go up and pour him a glass of water?'

'What about calling the cops?'

'That's up to Mr Kablunak.'

'It's on your hands, too.'

'Yeah?' Pascal scoffed. 'It won't be the hardest stain I got to wash off. What about you?' He pushed Jack into the back seat and slammed the door on him.

Walter started the car, looked over at his boss. 'Where to?'

'De Groot Galleries,' said Kablunak, eyes still closed.

Walter swung the Mercedes around and headed back towards the city. Jack looked out of the window, tired and resigned. All he knew was that he would not be climbing into bed with Kim again any time soon. And there was a dead man's ten grand in his pocket.

'Could we drive by my place?' he said. 'I need to feed my cat.'

Eyes still closed, Kablunak said: 'Sixty-eight percent

of domestic animals die from obesity-related disease, Mr Susko.'

'Is that a no?'

They wound through Rose Bay, Double Bay, then turned up Ocean Street in Edgecliff. Kablunak had *Relaxin' with the Miles Davis Quintet*, 1956, on the stereo. Jack had to admit the man had taste. The sky was uneven in its darkness: the last remnants of night were choked with clouds, beginning to move and churn, black folding into edges of grey and steely shadows curling and twisting like plumes of smoke. It really was going to bucket down, any moment. Jack checked the thought: it was going to come down all right, and it was going to be all over his head.

Something thudded, as though the rear wheels of the Merc had hit a pothole. Jack noticed Walter glance into the rear-view mirror.

'Was that him?' said Fat Boy.

'Yeah,' said Pascal. 'Should we give him a drink or something?'

'He's been in there for a while.'

Kablunak tapped his leg, following the music.

'Who?' asked Jack, slightly concerned.

'It'll be pretty hot in there by now, too,' said Walter.

A couple more dull thuds came from the boot. Jack could feel the vibrations through the seat, right in his kidneys. 'Who have you got in the back? Shane?' he asked, voice a touch strained. The idea made him feel a little queasy. *Jesus.*

'It's not fucking Shane,' said Pascal.

'Do not be so concerned, Mr Susko.' Kablunak sounded

bored. 'I let Mr Ferguson go ...' He paused. 'Days ago.'

'What, from a moving car?'

The Russian smiled. 'I am not the KGB, Mr Susko. We dropped him off at the Royal Prince Alfred, as a matter of fact. Emergency ward. Unfortunately, there was a very full waiting room and the blood was coming.' He shrugged his shoulders. 'But, you know, only a broken nose.' Kablunak reached down and massaged his leg, just above the knee. 'I asked him to keep out of my way for a while. Maybe he moved to Melbourne?'

Jack shifted in his seat, the leather creaking expensively. 'So who's looking after your spare wheel?'

'Your cousin, Mr Susko. Who else?'

Jack let the news sink in. 'Right,' he said. 'Of course.' A couple of pellets of rain hit the windscreen, but that was it. 'You know him, too, then?'

'Not at all, Mr Susko. He opened the door at Mr Ferguson's house when we knocked.' The Russian looked out into the street. 'And now he knows *me*. And that is far more important.'

'You went around to Shane's house?' Jack was thinking about Kim. 'What for?'

'We were looking for you, Mr Susko. Walter here recognised the girl at your shop earlier. Shane's flatmate, no? It was an interesting coincidence.' The Russian adjusted something on the air-conditioning. 'I am always wary of interesting coincidences.'

'You didn't do anything to her?'

'Of course not, Mr Susko. We are not the barbarian hordes. The young lady was asleep. And your cousin, as you can no doubt imagine, was quite willing to talk to us.

It was unnecessary to wake her.'

Jack felt a moment of relief. 'What are you going to do with Carl?'

'Oh, just keep him handy for a moment. I worry that too many people already know about my Bible, Mr Susko.' He gave Walter a look: it was firmly in the territory of unpleasant. 'And maybe I will convince your cousin to forget about it? That a life of crime is not a worthwhile career pursuit. Especially if you stumble onto the path of my career.'

'That's very kind of you. I think he might be getting the idea right about now.'

'Yes. I believe you are correct.'

Walter turned the Mercedes into Queen Street, Woollahra.

'Ah. Here we are,' said Viktor Kablunak. 'Let us go and visit Lewis. See if we cannot help Mr Susko out of his *predicament.*'

~28~

As it was still very early, Walter immediately found a spot when he turned off Queen and into Spicer Street, opposite an empty café with a *For Lease* sign in the window and an old faded poster for last year's Sydney French Film Festival. As Walter parked the Mercedes, Jack thought of Monica Bellucci. Unfortunately the thought did not last for long. The street was the same one he had turned into last Friday in the Toyota, when the whole damn thing had started. Except now it was early morning instead of late afternoon. And the wheels were slightly more expensive. And this time, he was arriving at De Groot Galleries *with* the heist guys instead of meeting them there. And his cousin was in the boot of the car, too. It was like some *Twilight Zone* game of opposites.

Hell, he even had ten thousand dollars in his pocket, instead of the three-twenty in change he had jingling around in there the week before.

He unclipped the seatbelt, took a deep breath. Life was strange and turned on a five-cent coin. That fact had always buoyed him in his darker moments: but right now it was more a cause for concern. Jack hoped it did not mean he was going to come out a little more cynical down the other end. Lois usually handled all that stuff, and more than well enough for the two of them.

'He can stay where he is,' said Kablunak to Walter, pointing with his thumb to the rear of the car. 'Just wait here until we get back.' He opened the door and stepped into the street.

The air was thick and wet, not the slightest edge of morning freshness to it. The sky was a bunched-up blanket of gloom. Jack, Kablunak and Pascal walked down Spicer Street, turned into Peaker Lane, walked a little further and then descended the concrete driveway into the car park beneath De Groot Galleries. A black BMW 120i was parked in one of the spaces.

'Looks like somebody's here,' said Pascal, checking out the Beamer. 'Might be better not to just waltz in.'

Kablunak nodded in agreement. 'Gun,' he said.

Pascal reached behind him and took out the .38 snubnose that was wedged in his belt. He flipped open the barrel, checked the chambers and gave them a spin. Just like in the movies. Jack pulled his bag further up his shoulder. As much as he did not like guns — or at least not those that were pointed at him — the precise, thick-sounding, cold metal click-clack of the weapon in Pascal's hand was strangely satisfying. Reassuring. He almost asked if he could hold it for a moment. Or if maybe he could borrow it for the rest of the day.

They walked over to a scratched service door: there was a picture of a staircase on it.

'After you, Mr Susko,' said Viktor Kablunak.

'What are we actually going to do up there?'

The Russian levelled his cold eyes at Jack. 'We are going to stop all of this nonsense, Mr Susko.'

'Oh, good.'

'And then you will be in my debt.'

'What about my book?'

'*From Russia with Love*? I accept it as a small token of your gratitude.'

Pascal gave Jack a push. 'In.'

Jack went through the door and started up the stairs. Pascal and the Russian followed. They climbed to the top, went through another door and entered a hallway. Jack remembered that the room he had been tied up in — the one with the safe in it — was on the left. The gallery was on the right. He went right, walked about ten metres, and then paused before the door that led into the smaller gallery room. He could hear voices. He strained his ears and listened for a moment. Larissa was talking: he could not understand exactly what she was saying, but she did not sound too distressed. Jack turned to Kablunak and Pascal, shrugged his shoulders and gave them a questioning look. Pascal put a finger to his lips, then pointed at the door with his gun. Silently mouthed: *You go*. Then he pointed to the other door in the hallway, the one that Jack remembered led to the kitchen. Pascal motioned with his head, indicating that he and Kablunak would go in there. Jack now gave them a perplexed look and held his hands up, to show that he was at a loss as to what they were on about, but Pascal and Viktor had already ducked away through the kitchen door and half closed it silently behind them.

He stared after them, now alone in the dark, empty corridor. That was their plan? They were going to hide in the kitchen? *Jesus*.

Behind him, the gallery door opened. Jack stood in a beam of light. It threw a very long shadow of him down the hallway: elongated legs slightly apart, ten-foot-long orang-utan arms and hands by his sides, everything stretched up to a ridiculously compacted head and shoulders and torso. He stood there, staring at the image, like a black cut-out on the floor.

'The fuck are you doing, Susko?'

Jack waited for Pascal to step back out into the hallway again with the .38 and start waving it around a little. After a couple of seconds, it was clear that this was not going to happen. He waited a few moments more, just in case. Nothing.

'Susko,' said Lewis behind him. 'I thought I asked you to call. You shouldn't sneak around like that, you know?' He stepped forward out of the doorway and stuck a gun into Jack's kidneys. 'It's a good way to get dead.'

Jack held his breath and put his hands up. He had no idea what Plan A was, so how the hell was he supposed to put Plan B into motion?

~*29*~

Outside, thunder cracked and the rain began to pour in a roaring rush.

'In here,' said Lewis. Then, with a smirk in his voice: 'And you can put your fucking hands down.'

Jack turned, dropping his arms. He was surprised to see Lewis in a black suit. Tight around his shoulders and chest, as though maybe it was a size too small: or maybe Lewis was just always a size too big, no matter what he wore. He looked a little hot: beads of sweat had gathered at his temples. Underneath the jacket, a white shirt and a thin black tie that seemed to be struggling to find a neck somewhere below his blonde, concrete-block head. Jack looked down at Lewis' shoes and noticed how small his feet were. He thought about mentioning the old correlation between shoe size and manhood, but decided it was probably better to wait until Lewis was no longer pointing a gun at him.

The big man stepped aside and Jack walked through the door. In the gallery, things did not look as Jack had expected them to. He paused, hitched his bag over his shoulder.

'Bit early for booze, isn't it?'

Larissa Tate was sitting on the edge of Rhonda de Groot's desk. She was wearing a charcoal-grey pinstriped suit with a pencil skirt, tight around her smooth thighs and ending just where her exquisitely chiselled knees began. Under the jacket, a pale-pink blouse with a ruffle front, and a thin, silver chain around her neck. Her high heels were sideways on the floor below her feet, as though kicked off after a hard day at the office. She was sipping from a champagne flute: no doubt a very fine, biscuity French number. Two orange-labelled bottles were on the desk beside her and neither was wearing their cork.

Larissa smiled brightly, her face welcoming and warm. 'Jack! You're already here.' She slid off the desk and tugged at her skirt as she looked up at him. 'That's great.' Under the perfect, straight fringe, her big browns were like a couple of chocolate-coated almonds. She turned and grabbed one of the bottles on the desk and topped up her glass. 'Would you like a drink?' she asked, as though Jack had arrived for a gallery opening. 'Come on, have one. Join us.'

He took it all in. Larissa and Lewis. Dressed like a couple of account executives. He noticed two small leather suitcases upright and side-by-side in the corner beside the desk. A matching pair: *His* and *Hers*. Oh yeah. Jack took it all in.

'Off somewhere?' he said.

Larissa glanced at him sideways. 'Business trip, Jack. To do some business.'

'Someplace nice?'

'Yes. Someplace nice.'

'Hotel or do you know people?'

'Hotel. And I know people.'

'Good stolen art and money-laundering service?'

She grinned. 'The best.'

'Then you're all set.'

'So have a drink and wish me well.'

Jack noticed the *me*. He turned to Lewis, watched him a moment, but Mr Muscles did not notice anything.

'Jack?' said Larissa. 'You want some champagne or what?'

'Got anything stronger?'

'Champagne only, lover boy. Relax. You don't have to be such a man all the time.' She glanced at Lewis. 'It can get really boring.'

Jack stared at Larissa Tate. Questions tumbled into his brain and tried to settle into the slots, like a hundred roulette balls bouncing around on the same wheel. 'Champagne will have to do then,' he said.

'Coming right up.'

Okay. So it was Larissa and Lewis. Rhonda, Jack, Shane and Carl, all scratched. Kablunak was in the kitchen. Richard de Groot was dead. Somebody had killed him. *Who?* They had sped away in the Maserati. *Maybe.* Most likely. *But not necessarily.* But … *Shit.* Jack looked at Lewis, holding a gun. Too obvious? Jack had no idea. Somebody had pulled the trigger — and that was the somebody he wanted to watch out for.

He remembered a line from the 1963 bestseller *Tuesday*

and There's No Tomorrow by Francis O'Connor: 'Count the bullets before you move, and make sure you count 'em all the way to six. And if you can't count, brother … you'd better wait for Christmas.'

Lewis went over to a plush, red two-seater sofa pushed up against the wall opposite Jack. He sat down, heavily, leaned back and rested one squat tree-trunk leg on top of the other. He held the gun in his hand loose, only casually aimed at Jack. With his other hand, he grabbed some nuts out of a cut-glass bowl resting on the arm of the sofa and shoved them into his mouth.

Jack said: 'So where's Rhonda?'

Lewis laughed. Peanut shrapnel flew out of his mouth. 'Never heard of her.'

'Is that what you're going to tell the cops?' Jack was making it up as he went along.

'Fuck off,' scoffed Lewis, screwing up his face. 'What cops?'

'The ones I've called.'

'You haven't called any fucking cops.'

'Yeah? What if I said they were out in the kitchen right now?'

Lewis shook his head, leaned it back against the sofa and then draped an arm over his eyes. 'Don't make me get up, Susko. You've got nothing. Zilch.'

Larissa walked over and handed Jack a glass of champagne. She stood with her back to Lewis. 'Pay no attention to him,' she said. 'He's drunk.'

'I'm not fucking drunk!'

Larissa stared intently at Jack and frowned a little. Then she smiled and brought her glass up to her lips. 'You could still change your mind,' she said, softly, so that Lewis could not hear.

'You're crazy.'

'What are you whispering?' growled Lewis.

Larissa smiled again and then gave Jack a quick, disappointed, *oh-well-bad-luck* kind of look. She winked at him and tapped his glass with her own. Jack stared at her and swallowed some champagne. Then he swallowed some more and finished it off. He could smell her perfume, a sophisticated, vaguely floral scent that added a good whiff of boardroom sex to her strictly business look.

He pointed at Mr Muscles on the sofa and handed his glass back to Larissa. 'Are you going to tell me about it?'

'What's to tell?' Larissa moved away, sipped more of her champagne as she walked. She turned around and sat back against the edge of the desk. 'Jack plus the mail plus the Sergius equals flight to Spain and fortune. And here you are.'

'You use a calculator for all that or did you do it in your head?'

'Very funny, Jack.'

'So how come you're here so early, all dressed up and raring to go?'

She smiled and turned to face him. 'There's been other business to attend to, Jack.' Larissa pointed to a laptop on the desk. 'While we sleep, the rest of the world does business.'

'Getting the buyer ready, huh?'

'Good boy. Full marks. There's an art thief in you somewhere, eh?' She sighed. 'See how good we could be together?'

'You still haven't got the Sergius.'

'But you're here, Susko,' said Lewis from the couch, slurring his South African accent a little. 'So we do.'

'The mailman doesn't deliver this early.'

'Oh come on, Jack. So then why are you here?' Larissa shook her head. 'You've had it the whole time, haven't you? Tricky boy. Probably under your bed the other night.' She gave him a sultry look.

Jack stopped. It was a good moment for Kablunak and Pascal to come bursting through the door. They did not. He stared at Larissa. He checked out Lewis again on the sofa. The two of them actually thought he had the Bible there with him. What the hell was he going to do now?

'Poor Jack,' said Larissa. 'You had your chance, love. I even threw myself at you. And I was good. How much bait does a healthy man need?'

'Fuck all, baby!' Lewis lifted his head, threw more nuts into his mouth and chewed them, grinning like an idiot. Jack noticed that the gun was now aimed at a painting on the wall down by his right. Might be another perfect moment for Kablunak and Pascal to come bursting into the room. He hoped for a second or two longer, but nothing happened. Maybe they were making a toasted sandwich.

Larissa said: 'It was nice, Jackie-o. You were lovely. But of course, that was also when I knew. You're not game enough, Jack, not really. You're a lot of talk and pose, and it's all very nice and fun and looks good, but you'd never take it over the line.'

'What, like kill somebody?' Jack watched for her reaction.

She ignored the comment, as though she had not heard it. 'You flirt on the edges, but you're too cautious. Women need *commitment*, a man who'll go the full distance. I should have known with you after the first time, but I must have believed there was a chance. Or maybe I was just hoping.'

'Commitment?' Jack frowned. 'Have I slipped into a parallel universe or something?'

'You've got a spark, baby, but ...' Larissa looked meaningfully at him and shook her pretty head. She held the look for a moment and Jack could feel her driving it home. 'I did, honey,' she said, with a little swoon in her voice for added effect. 'For a moment I hoped. But then I knew. You're just another scaredy cat. Jack who plays pretend, but never the real thing.' She drank some of her champagne.

Jack felt his body fill with tiredness. Outside, the rain was getting louder: the streets splashed and the streetlights blurred, and the drains and gutters flooded. The parched city drank its fill.

Larissa grinned. 'Have I hurt your feelings, Mr Susko?'

'I'm devastated,' he said, face grim but not because of what she had said. He nodded at Lewis. 'He knows you're going to do him over, doesn't he?'

'You don't get it, do you, Jack?'

'You think he does?'

Lewis did not like being talked about as though he was not there. 'Enough of that shit,' he said, a dose of menace in his tone. He tried to sit up, but it was all just too much effort. He fell back into the sofa and stretched his legs and flicked the gun at Jack a couple of times, casually. 'The Sergius, Susko. Now.'

Larissa smiled at Jack as though he was a cheeky five-year-old. 'Come on now. You win some, you lose some,' she said and held out her hand. She pointed at his bag, slung behind his hip. 'You lose some.'

'That the hand you used to shoot Richard de Groot?'

That one got her. 'What?'

'Or did you just pack the cash into a bag while Lewis let him have it?'

The South African looked up. 'The fuck you talking about?'

Jack watched their faces: the surprise seemed genuine enough. But he was not putting any money down yet. 'I saw him about an hour ago,' he said. 'Two plugs in the back. Head down in the floor safe. Safe empty.'

'Fuck!' Lewis had managed to get off the sofa this time.

'That the gun, Lewis?' asked Jack.

The big man ignored him, looked at Larissa. 'She shot him. Just like she said she would.'

'Who?' But Jack knew as soon as he asked. *Rhonda.*

Larissa stared into space. She had lost a little colour in her face.

'We've got to get out of here,' said Lewis. He had sobered up in record time. 'Right now.'

'Not without the Sergius.'

Lewis swung around and pointed the gun at Jack. 'Okay. Give. Now.'

'I told you. I haven't got it.'

'What?' Larissa almost growled. Jack was glad she was not holding the gun. 'Where the fuck is it?'

'Post office,' he said, feeling his legs go a little cold. 'Waiting to be picked up.' He swallowed and held the strap of his bag. 'I've got the slip but you're going to have to wait for nine o'clock.'

'The post office!' Lewis was shaking his head. 'Babe,

we've got to go right now. There's no time for the post office.'

'We're going to go get it,' said Larissa.

'Fuck the Sergius!' Lewis pointed his gun at the suitcases in the corner. 'There's two hundred grand in there!'

Jack looked at the suitcases. So they had stolen the money. And then Rhonda had come around for the killing deed.

Larissa blinked, came back from wherever she had gone. 'What are we going to do with two hundred thousand dollars, you moron? That's nowhere near enough! I'm not planning on getting a fucking job!'

'Yeah, well it's enough for me.' Lewis swung the gun around at Jack again. 'Pick up the bags, Susko. We're going down to the car.'

'Don't be an idiot.' Larissa moved over to stand in the way.

'Hey! We did the safe and now he's dead! How long do you think it's going to take the cops to be onto us? We've got to go, *now*.'

'We took the money so that we could move the Bible,' said Larissa, rigid and pissed off and just holding it all in. 'Without the Bible, the money is nothing. Does that fucking compute?'

'I'm out of here.'

'You stupid fuck.'

Lewis stopped. Stared at Larissa. Wiggled a few fingers on the hand holding the gun.

'You wouldn't dare,' she said.

'Want to find out?'

Jack was wondering if he should call out for Kablunak.

'Which post office?' snapped Larissa, swinging around to Jack again, not concerned with the gun.

'City. Corner of York and Market.'

'Morning peak hour into the city!' cried Lewis. 'Come on, it's fucking pointless.'

'Shut up.'

The gallery door swung open behind Jack. He turned, relieved, expecting to see Pascal and Viktor Kablunak.

He expected wrong.

~*30*~

MAX THE GALLERY ASSISTANT WAS THERE — with a gun. It looked a little too big for him, but he held it with a certain professional nonchalance and style: both hands around the stock, stretched out in front of him about shoulder high, sweeping the barrel swiftly across the room, and then pausing and holding it steady on Lewis. Max was wearing a Hawaiian shirt, just like the first time Jack had seen him, only this one was blue with lots of Hula girls all over it. His bare legs looked like the meat had been boiled off them. In his whiny little voice, he said: 'Nobody fucking move.'

He might not have looked it but Max sounded pretty serious.

Rhonda de Groot walked in behind him. 'Well, well, well,'

she said. 'Everybody in, nice and early.' She was smiling, but not like she was happy.

Lewis still had the gun in his hand, but had not adapted quickly to the new situation.

'Drop it, big boy,' said Max.

'What?' Lewis gave a confused look, like he had just seen a magic trick and was trying to work it out. Then he bent his knees a little and dropped the gun to the ground. As reality hit home further, his drink-warmed complexion rapidly paled.

Rhonda de Groot stood as though she was staring down at everybody from a pulpit. Her womanly curves stretched defiantly against the tight fabric of her maroon designer tracksuit. A white Nike headband matched her white Nike sneakers. She looked fit, fifty and fucked off. 'Where is the Sergius? And where is my husband's money?'

Jack saw Larissa glance at her handbag on the desk. Lewis crossed his arms. Lifted his chin at Rhonda de Groot. 'You shot him.'

'Technically, no.' Rhonda patted Max's shoulder, smiling. 'My little dynamo was there to take care of all that.'

'You killed your husband for Christ's sake!' Lewis was having trouble coming to terms with the news.

'And?'

'What?' Lewis's mouth moved to expand on his confusion, but nothing came out. His eyes were glazed with drink and shock. He closed them and cleared his throat, loudly, and then looked at Rhonda de Groot again and tried to appear determined and tough. 'All right,' he said. 'I don't care. If you want the truth, I don't give a shit. I've always hated him. But what the fuck do you think you're going to do now?'

Rhonda let it out as a motherly sigh. 'My main concern at the moment is you.' She looked at Larissa over by the desk. 'And your *deceit*.'

'What do you want? An apology?'

'Oh, if only an apology was all that was necessary, Lew,' said Rhonda. 'I just don't know that I'll ever be able to trust you again.'

'Trust *me*? You're a lunatic!' He shook his head, looked at Larissa and then at Jack, as though for support. 'Christ, I should have picked it the other day. In the middle of the fucking city, shooting a gun off in Susko's bookshop!' Lewis warmed up, indignant. He reached for his neck and loosened his already flaccid tie. 'I kept you out of trouble and now you've got this midget pointing a fucking gun at me.'

Max adjusted the aim of his gun. 'Need those nuts?'

'I've been stressed, Lew,' said Rhonda. 'You know that.'

'Yeah, I *know* it.'

Larissa said: 'You killed Richard? Now, after all these years?'

Rhonda put her hands on her hips, stretched out her right leg and tapped her foot on the floor a couple of times as she slightly bent her left knee. She counted, softly: *one, two, three* … Then she stood and changed legs. 'That was your fault, my dear. I was so *angry* when Richard opened the safe and there was nothing there. Plus the fact that I was already upset with Lewis here, going behind my back.'

'How did you find out?' snapped Lewis.

Max grinned. 'Like following an elephant through a meadow.'

'You little faggot.'

The gun moved up. Max glanced at Rhonda, his face grim, asking for permission. Jack tensed, sure he would get it.

'That's offensive, Lew,' said Rhonda. 'I've told you before.'

'There's nothing going on between me and Larissa.' Lewis swore. 'It's just business.'

'Everybody knows she's a slut,' said Rhonda. 'I'm sure even Richard was —'

'Christ, just listen! I couldn't handle your moods anymore, all right? I wanted out, no more fucking de Groots in my life. You get it?'

'You could have talked to me about it.' Her sincerity was thin as fairy floss.

'Oh come off it!'

'You said you were going to help me. You promised. The Sergius, the money, a new life. What happened, Lew?'

Lewis looked at Rhonda de Groot with disgust, his eyes filled with hate. 'Games. Just fucking games, that's all. And that's all finished now.'

'You ungrateful fucking *shit*. I got you out of South Africa, I got Richard to take you on again after you got out of jail, and what do you go and do? Hook up with this little Australian *slapper*.'

Jack looked at Larissa: to his surprise, she appeared somewhat amused.

'I'm not your lackey,' said Lewis, venom hot in his voice. 'You and your arrogant husband, think you can just tell me what to do?' He made a sound as though he was about to spit. 'Well, not anymore. Those days are over. He's dead and I'm taking the cash and you can go to hell.'

Rhonda grinned, hands back on hips. 'Unbelievable. Richard always said you were too stupid for anything.'

'I've had about as much shit as I'm going to take from you.' His voice wavered a little at the edges.

Rhonda ignored him and glanced around the gallery. 'Where's the money from Richard's safe?' Before anybody could answer, she saw the suitcases in the corner by the desk. 'Ah, there we are. Good.' She turned back to Lewis. 'How much did you find in the end?'

The thick man hesitated. 'Two hundred thousand.'

'In the floor safe?'

'And the one in the bedroom.'

Rhonda grinned. 'Good old Richard.'

Lewis pointed his chin, raised a little bit of eyebrow. 'So now what?'

'Now?' replied Rhonda, as though she was confused by what he had said. 'Now nothing, Lew.'

She reached for the gun in Max's hand, pointed it at Lewis and before he or anybody else knew what the hell was going on, she fired. Once. Twice. Thrice. The rain pummelling the gallery windows drowned out some of the noise, but it was still very loud. Jack's ears were ringing as the blonde muscle man took the bullets in his chest, where they thudded and buried themselves deep. He fell heavily into the sofa: his head snapped back and then instantly bounced forward off the cushioned velour, and then lifted up again, but not as far, and then fell and wobbled a little and finally rested on his chest. Dead.

'Max,' said Rhonda de Groot as she turned to face Larissa, pointing the gun. 'Could you please get me a glass of water?'

~31~

JACK HAD ALWAYS SUSPECTED that giving up smoking was going to be the death of him: but had he known it was actually going to be at the hands of a mad, gun-wielding, middle-aged South African gallery owner, he would never have quit.

Rhonda de Groot stood perfectly still, smooth blue smoke drifting around her, eyes locked on Larissa, the gun ready to speak again but holding its tongue for the moment.

The storm outside emptied over the city. Soon enough, everything would be washed and clean and sparkling anew beneath the soft sunrise, and the gentle morning would herald a forgiven day. Everywhere, except maybe at De Groot Galleries, Queen Street, Woollahra.

Jack glanced at the door without moving his head, wondered how Max was getting on in the kitchen. No sounds that he could hear — but then the rain was hitting everything hard and his ears were still ringing from the gun blasts. What the hell was Kablunak doing?

'Champagne, Rhonda?' said Larissa. Somehow, she managed to sound smug, as though *she* was holding the gun and not the other way around. She turned to the desk and picked up the bottle there, shaking it a little to see if there was anything left. 'Might take the edge off, huh?'

'You made him do it, didn't you?'

'Would that make you feel better, Rhonda?'

'I know you did.'

'He was a grown man.'

'You made him do it.'

Larissa held the glass of champagne she had poured for Rhonda de Groot up and then placed it on the desk. 'The problem with you, Rhonda, is that you *think* the world is how you'd like to see it. An affliction of the rich, I suspect. But reality just doesn't work like that.'

'Lewis was stupid and vulnerable. He hated Richard and you saw how you could use him. And now they're both dead. Because of you.'

'I think maybe that gun in your hand has got more to do with it, Rhonda.'

'You *slut*. What did you promise him?'

Larissa poured herself some more champagne. She sipped. Then she looked up at Rhonda through her fringe of shiny brown hair. Her eyes were narrowed, lips pursed. 'The opportunity to get the hell away from you. What else?'

Rhonda stretched her gun arm out a little further,

shortened the distance between its barrel and Larissa's body. Jack felt his heart pounding like an air compressor in his chest. He was close enough to tackle Rhonda, but the gun would go off before he could get hold of it.

'Don't look so shocked,' said Larissa. 'Why would he like *you*? What, just because you're his sister?'

Jack looked at Rhonda de Groot in disbelief. 'He's your brother?'

'That's right,' said Larissa. 'Her own flesh and blood. I wonder what the Sergius would have to say about it? Straight down, bottom floor. The hot place.'

'And you?' snapped Rhonda, the gun trembling a little in her hand.

'I'm in it for the money, sister. I haven't killed anybody for it and neither the money nor the Sergius belongs to anybody either.' Larissa looked at Jack. 'I might have tried to lead the odd person astray, but nobody complained, far as I can tell.'

'You started all this. You came into my family and drove the wedge between us.'

'Yeah, Rhonda. Simple as that. I've been planning it for years.'

'You convinced Richard to steal the Sergius from Viktor, didn't you?'

Larissa sighed.

'Answer me!'

'I didn't even know about the fucking Sergius,' she said, voice rising in volume.

'No. It was you. He'd stopped all that. He told me.'

'Well, he told *me* that it was going to be the easiest three million he had ever made. Plus the bonus of annoying

Viktor Kablunak.'

Rhonda was staring into space now, eyes vacant as her mind shuffled the cards, but obviously a few were falling out of the pack. Jack swallowed. Braced. Locked his eyes on the gun.

'And for the record,' said Larissa, coolly topping up her glass again. 'I've never been attracted to short-arse men.'

The gun in Rhonda's hand recoiled: the sound was like a thousand Rottweilers barking in the same split second. The champagne glass in Larissa's hand hit the floor. Jack shuddered as the force of the bullet split the air in the gallery, and the blast reverberated and bounced off the walls. More bitter gun smoke drifted into his nostrils and burned his eyes, and the thought of Larissa taking the bullet sifted in slow motion through his mind. He turned to look and was relieved to see she was still standing.

Larissa had cupped a hand over her left ear. Blood seeped out between her fingers and down her long smooth neck. And there was a funny look on her face, as though she was trying to remember what she had just been talking about.

Jack said: 'Jesus, are you all right?'

She looked at her hand, then gently patted around her ear. Her eyes widened. 'You shot my ear lobe off,' she said, as though in a dream; shock was obviously still holding back the pain information from her brain.

Rhonda de Groot adjusted the gun slightly, not quite believing that Larissa was still on her feet. 'You lucky little *bitch*.'

All of Jack's senses were brimming, and then he knew the gun was going to go off again. In the moment it fired, Jack lunged with his shoulder and knocked Rhonda de Groot sideways. She screamed and swung the gun around. As they fell, she landed it, hard and clean, right on the side of his head, just above the ear. He groaned and tried to reach for her wrist. Hot sparks flashed through his skull. *Fuck.* After the last time, he knew he should have worn a goddamn helmet.

Rhonda yelled and flayed with the gun. 'Get off me!' She pulled the trigger and shot off another round. Jack flinched but did not feel any bullets hit. As he wrestled Rhonda onto her back, Pascal burst through the door.

'What the fuck?'

He took in the scene and then ran over and grabbed the gun out of Rhonda's hand. He dragged her away by the arm, a metre or two across the carpet.

'Let go of me you son of a bitch!'

Over by the desk, Larissa started to laugh. Blood had spread down one side of her head and neck and into the collar of her pinstriped suit jacket. She laughed and her body shook. After a few seconds, she calmed down a little. Then she reached into her handbag on the desk and pulled out a travel-pack of tissues.

For a moment, it was all held breaths in the gallery. Then one long exhale. And the rain beat down and soothed the world and slowly drained the room of its drama.

~*32*~

JACK LAY ON THE CARPET AND THEN ROLLED onto his back. Stared at the ceiling. Reached up and delicately felt the side of his head where Rhonda's gun had kissed it. A smooth bump pulsed with pain. There were two bumps now. He decided to stay where he was for the moment and hoped everyone else would just go home.

Viktor Kablunak walked in. His hands were in his pockets: casual, relaxed. He looked around, nodded a couple of times, then angled his head down and stared at Jack on the floor. He grinned. 'You have done well, Mr Susko,' he said. 'Only one dead body.'

'Not enough for you?'

Kablunak cleared his throat. 'Plenty.'

Jack closed his eyes. 'You took your time, Viktor. What the hell were you waiting for? A phone call?'

'Our friend Max is a tenacious little man.'

Pascal made a noise in his throat. 'I'd rather stick a ferret down my pants.'

'Yes. But he is secure now. And besides, I never interfere in domestic disputes, Mr Susko. They are ... *private* affairs. This is one of the main problems in the world today, I believe.' He looked up, squinted into the middle distance and sucked at his teeth. 'I have many thoughts on this subject.'

'Boss,' said Pascal, holding Rhonda's arm. 'We've got to get out of here.'

Kablunak nodded vaguely, then stared down at his shoes and took a few meandering steps. The windows of the gallery were thick with the fug of sweat and gun smoke and death.

'The line between the private and the public domain has been ... *eroded*,' continued the Russian. 'Political correctness has instilled a false morality in us, Mr Susko. But really, it is for small minds and the self-righteous, this *P-C*, as they call it. An excuse to stick their noses everywhere they should not. They cannot admit that what they find impossible to fathom is that their lives are not grand statements or world-changing examples of what is right or what should be. No no no ...' He wagged a finger. 'They are ... *stupid* people. Deep down they know that they are nothing, and will do nothing, and will die *nothing*. Better the old ways, Mr Susko. When one had a *private life*. The home, the family. Where a man could be king and a woman queen. Where no other laws could reign.' The Russian smiled. He turned to Rhonda de Groot, standing defiantly beside Pascal. 'Isn't that right, Rhonnie?'

Richard de Groot's widow scoffed, amused. 'Still full of shit, Viktor,' she said, her voice clipped and precise and all settled down now after the drama. 'Why doesn't that surprise me?'

Kablunak's face darkened. He paused, held what he was about to say in his mouth for a moment. He walked over to a painting on the wall to his right, clasped his hands behind his back and inspected the picture. Then he said: 'Shooting your brother dead, Rhonda. Why doesn't that surprise *me*?'

'And her husband.' Jack had got up off the floor. Thunder cracked, hard and loud, like a mountain splitting in two. Lightning flashed in the fogged-up gallery window, blurred by the flooding sky. Outside, the world was black and pale grey, glimmering like an old movie reel that had been played a few too many times. Nothing was clear: inside or out.

'So it was you,' said Kablunak.

Rhonda reached up and brushed at her hair. 'Go to hell, Viktor.'

The Russian gave her a sad look. 'Dear Rhonda. What has become of you? And what will become of you now?'

'All alone,' added Larissa.

'You little slut!' she yelled suddenly, lunging towards Larissa. Her expression was set to *if-looks-could-kill*. Pascal held her back. 'She made me kill my brother!'

Larissa dabbed at her ear with a bunch of tissues. 'Lewis hated your guts,' she said.

'I raised him from the age of four!'

'Well done. You should write a guide.'

Jack watched Rhonda's face turn deep red: then, just as quickly, she reined in her anger and visibly calmed down.

She stretched herself taller. 'I know about you and Richard,' she said, her tone full of pomp and something like pride.

'What?' replied Larissa, and grimaced, as though she had bitten something sour. 'You're delusional. Fucking men to get what you want, that's your generation, Rhonda, not mine. We hardly need 'em at all these days.'

'You're lying.'

'Oh, come on!' Larissa looked at Kablunak. 'She needs her medication.'

'Mr Kablunak?' said Pascal with some urgency. He nodded towards the door.

Viktor checked his watch. 'Yes. We really must go.' He looked up at Jack and gestured towards the hallway door. 'Shall we?'

'What do you want to do with these guys?' Pascal sounded concerned.

'Leave them. This is a family affair. Nothing to do with me.' Kablunak narrowed his eyes at Larissa and pointed at the suitcases in the corner. 'Is that Richard's money?'

Larissa closed her eyes and nodded.

'Good,' said the Russian as he turned away. 'Pascal. Bring the suitcases.'

'You just going to let everybody go?'

'I can be a sporting man at times, Pascal. The police will find everything they need to make their arrests.' He grinned. 'Or maybe Miss Tate and Mrs de Groot could team up for their escape? Give the police something to do?'

Larissa reached for the champagne bottle on the desk. She picked it up and took a swig. 'Can I borrow some of the cash, Viktor?'

'No.'

Jack was watching Larissa: there was something about the way she and Kablunak had spoken to one another. 'Can I ask a question?' he said.

'Make it brief, Mr Susko.'

'When your boys busted in last Friday. How'd you know the Sergius was here? In the safe?'

Viktor Kablunak raised his eyebrows a fraction. As though he was pleased. 'Very good, Mr Susko.'

'Same way you knew somebody would be here this morning, huh?'

The Russian smiled, amused now.

Rhonda de Groot leaned forward in Pascal's grip. She was thinking, intently, not sure where to look. Then she knew, and scowled at Larissa Tate. '*You*,' said the widow de Groot. 'You did it!'

Larissa tossed her hair and then pushed out her bottom lip and sent a quick breath up into her fringe, which waved for a second and then fell down again, perfectly in place, straight and silken. 'It's a bitch-eat-bitch world, Rhonda,' she said. 'Haven't you heard?'

Pascal's confusion turned into an itch in his underarm. He scratched, absently using the gun, looking from Larissa to Kablunak and then back again, like he was following a tennis match. But he had no idea what the score was.

Jack said: 'You know she's been planning to take the Sergius herself, don't you, Viktor?'

'Yes, Mr Susko. I have never been under any illusions when it comes to Miss Tate. That is why I am here.' His tone hardened a little. 'Enduring more fools. And all before my morning coffee.'

'Shall I order you one, Viktor?' asked Larissa. 'I think

Zigolini's might be open across the road.'

'Thank you, but no. I would hate for you to have to go out in the rain.'

She held out the bottle to him. 'Champagne then?'

'Please. I would prefer you enjoy it. While you can.'

Jack touched the side of his head, winced. 'What did you do to de Groot to make him come after you in the first place?' asked Jack, eyeing the Russian through his growing headache. He could not help but be intrigued by the man. And ... what else? *Impressed*?

'Didn't you know, Jack?' said Larissa. 'He sold him to the police back in South Africa.'

'We were left with nothing,' said Rhonda de Groot, bitterly.

Kablunak scoffed. 'You left with more than enough.'

'But with much less than they had,' said Larissa, as though she understood what Rhonda might have gone through, as though it was something worthy of a little sympathy.

'Business is business,' replied Kablunak. 'I was in a unique ... *situation*. And I needed to make a deal with the authorities.'

'About what?' asked Jack.

'Diamonds,' said Larissa, answering for the Russian. 'Mr *Kay* here and the now deceased Richard used to run rocks together.'

'He was never very good at it,' said Kablunak.

'So, eventually, Mr *Kay* sold him to the cops.'

'A simple case of *survival of the fittest*. They needed a criminal and I provided them with one. Hardly a problem. He only had to bribe his way out.'

'There was nothing left,' said Rhonda, softly and sadly. 'We came here with nothing.'

The Russian gave her a look of contempt. 'And for your sins, now you will have even less.'

'So de Groot wanted to get back at you by stealing the Sergius?'

Kablunak sighed. 'Revenge is an expensive, emotional, and ultimately unprofitable exercise. Look what it has cost him.'

'Much better spending your cash on insider trading,' said Larissa. Her tone was almost playful. 'Eh, Viktor?'

'Well, it is a calculated risk. But by the looks of things, I have got here just in time to protect my interests. No?'

Larissa smiled, shook her head with disappointment and then pointed at Jack. 'You know it's at the post office? He's had a pick-up slip for the thing the whole time. It's been sitting at the fucking post office for days.'

The Russian looked at Jack. Viktor Kablunak did not resemble Josef Stalin in the slightest, but his aura took on some of the menace and threat of the former dictator. 'This I did not know.'

Pascal frowned. 'He's had the fucking Sergius the whole fucking time?'

'The *whole* time,' said Larissa, with a mild version of glee.

'It is funny, Mr Susko,' said Kablunak. 'Out of everybody, I think it was you that I trusted the most.'

Jack shrugged. 'I just wanted my book back, Viktor. Making the best of a bad situation.'

'I understand. In fact, you show admirable qualities, Mr Susko.'

'So, a nice exchange, Viktor? As we had originally planned?' Jack was nervous but held it in as best he could. There was ten thousand dollars in his pocket. And if he could get his first edition back from the Russian, he might — even after all that had gone down — actually be *up*. Considering there were two bodies in the equation so far, that sounded pretty good to him. 'The Bible for the Bond,' he said.

'How the world turns,' said Kablunak. He spread his arms and looked around the gallery. 'There we were. And now here we are.'

'Crazy, isn't it?' said Larissa. She dropped the bloodied tissues onto the desk and reached into her handbag again. She rummaged around and then pulled something out. It was not a packet of fresh tissues. It was not a polka-dot handkerchief, either. Jack wondered how the hell she expected to blow her nose on it.

~*33*~

LARISSA PULLED THE TRIGGER and the gun jumped up in her hand. The bullet hit Pascal in the leg and he went down as though somebody had suddenly chopped it out from under him. Rhonda screamed and stumbled backwards. Pascal dropped his gun and grimaced and moaned loudly, as though he was about to clean and jerk two tonnes for the world record. He curled up on the floor and grabbed his thigh with both hands. He was panting like a woman between contractions, and his face glowed red with pain.

'Everybody against the back wall.'

Kablunak stared grimly at Larissa. 'If you have a brain, *mademoiselle*,' he said, 'I suggest that you use it.'

'Move it, Viktor.' Larissa took a single step towards him,

gun high. 'Don't think I wouldn't do it.'

The Russian stared hard at her, his mood foul, his eyes murderous. Tense seconds passed. Then he nodded and put his hands in the air.

'Now back it up. But not you, Jack. You stay right there.'

Christ. The side of Jack's head throbbed. The back of it and the frontal-lobe area, too. He watched Kablunak and Rhonda move to the rear wall. Pascal swore in a constant stream. Larissa waved the gun. 'Shut up. Sit.' Everybody sat. She hurried over to the two guns lying on the floor near Pascal, and with her stockinged foot she kicked them under the sofa and then retreated to the desk again. Still holding the gun on her prisoners, she leaned down and slipped her heels back onto her feet, right foot then left. She did this one-handed, strapped them on with skill and speed.

'Nice shoes,' said Jack. 'Not sure if they go with the bloody ear though.'

'Everything goes with Manolo Blahnik.' She straightened up. 'Now, how about you hand that postal slip over?'

'You're still going to go for the Sergius?'

Larissa held out an impatient hand. 'Don't make me shoot you.'

'The post office isn't even open.' Jack glanced at his watch. 'There's still over an hour to go.'

'Not your concern, Jackie-boy. Come on. I'm not going to ask you again.' She lifted the gun a little higher.

'Okay, okay.' Jack held up the palms of his hands. 'I've got to reach into my bag, is that all right?'

Larissa nodded.

'Think you'll pass as a Jack at the counter?'

'They never check the details with a pick-up slip.' She

smiled. 'And if they do, I'll just say I'm your wife.'

'What about the missing piece of your ear?'

'You bit it off making love to me.'

'There's blood all over your expensive jacket.'

'You had to take me just as I was about to leave for work.'

'Think they'll believe you?'

Larissa pointed the gun at Jack's bag, hanging by his hip. She frowned and flicked her fringe with agitation. 'Think you'll go to heaven because you died over an old Bible, Jack?'

He pulled his bag around and unbuckled the flap.

Pascal groaned, holding his leg. He was still coming to terms with what was going on: 'He had it the whole fucking time?' Nobody responded. 'Jesus *Christ*.'

Jack reached into his bag. He fished around. Felt things at his fingertips.

Pen.

Bus ticket.

Cigarette packet foil and plastic.

An old lighter.

Fuck.

Another old lighter.

Pencil.

USB plug.

Curls of lint in the corners and lining.

No postal slip.

Shit.

…

Kim?

Oh shit.

He did not panic immediately.

Jack stared at Larissa Tate. He pulled his naked hand out of the bag. He held it up, looked at it and turned it around a little, as though he was about to perform a card trick. When no ace appeared in his palm, Larissa frowned.

Woe the lowly second-hand bookseller.

~34~

Larissa was annoyed and in a hurry, so he gave her the abridged version. *Kim plus she's Shane's flatmate plus I was there last night plus postal slip in the bag equals she's got it.* It took a moment and a half to sink in. Then Larissa said: 'Fuck!'

Jack wondered where the bullet would hit him. He summoned all his magical powers, like a spoon-bender, and concentrated on his little finger, pointing it away from his body. They could do wonders with flesh-coloured plastic these days. But the gun remained silent. Larissa nodded. She already had another plan.

They locked Kablunak, Rhonda and Pascal in the windowless kitchen off the hallway at De Groot Galleries.

Max was already there, stuffed into one of the cupboards by Pascal. He had used Max's leather belt to secure the doors, slotted it through two handles and done it up tight. Pascal now tied a couple of tea towels around his leg to staunch the blood flow. Larissa had Jack strip everybody of mobile phones and keys. Rhonda swore and threatened and sobbed in between. Kablunak merely stared at Jack, his face serious, his eyes like tracer lights on a loaded gun: letting Jack know that what was happening was *not good*. That there would be repercussions. As Jack closed the door, he frowned and gave the Russian a look in return: *what the hell do you want me to do?* and left it at that.

Larissa found the first-aid kit in the storeroom and Jack cleaned her wound and stuck a band-aid on her ear while she kept the gun pointed at him: she was sitting down and made sure it was his balls that were in the firing line. For all the blood, it was just a small nick. *Lucky Larissa.* Jack wondered if she had used up her supplies. More worrying, though, were his own meagre reserves. The fuel warning light was flashing on his karma dashboard.

After that, she pulled the phone line out of the wall and tucked the phone under her arm and locked Jack in the storeroom. 'Just wait,' she said. Two, maybe three minutes later, she let him out again. Larissa had opened one of the suitcases and changed her bloodied clothes: now she was in tight jeans, a white long-sleeved T-shirt, and a pair of brown Campers.

'Getaway clothes?'

'Something like that.' She was hardly listening.

'What about a mask?'

'Shut up.'

She made him carry the two suitcases downstairs to the car park. The Maserati was two spaces along from the BMW. Larissa pointed the remote entry on her key ring and pressed the button. The BMW flashed its hazard lights.

'What's the time?' she asked.

Jack put one of the suitcases down beside the Beamer and looked at his watch. 'Nearly eight-thirty.'

'Good.'

'You know she's probably already there, waiting. Having a coffee and a muffin, watching the time at her leisure. And we've got peak hour. Whichever way you take.'

'We'll get there.' Larissa tossed him the car keys. 'Put those in the boot, then you drive.'

Jack stowed the suitcases then climbed into the driver's seat, Larissa waiting with the gun trained on him until he was strapped in and then got in herself. The car smelt of her perfume, and of plastic and leather newness, and of the yellow, flower-shaped deodoriser clipped to the ventilation louvres on the central console. Jack remembered the Toyota. *Fruits-of-the-goddamn-forest.*

'Careful over the ramp,' she said. 'It scrapes the rear.'

'And you're worried about that now?'

'Just watch it.'

Jack kicked the motor. He adjusted the driver's seat, sliding it back electronically. He checked and adjusted the mirrors and then drove slowly out of the car park. It had been a while since he used to drive the baddies around. He turned down Moncur Street, then left off the roundabout into Hargrave, straight through to Gurner and then took another left onto Glenmore Road.

'You think Oxford Street is wise?' asked Larissa, voice

edgy and irritated.

'Compared to what?'

'Jesus.' Larissa shook her head, looking through the windscreen. 'I'm not going to miss the fucking traffic in this town, that's for sure.'

The rain thrummed the car. It was getting hot inside with all the breathing and the adrenaline and the windows were fogging up. Jack got the demist going, front and rear, and set a little air blowing.

'So where are you headed? You already got a ticket booked?'

Larissa flicked her hair, distracted. 'When you've got cash, Jack, you've always got a ticket booked.' She combed her fringe with her fingers. 'And to think I might have been taking you with me.'

'I love Sydney too much.'

'You love scraping a living in ones and twos? Living alone with a cat? Driving a Toyota?'

'I don't have the Toyota anymore. And I only get ones. And leave Lois out of it.'

'It's your life.'

He glanced at the weapon in her hand: for the moment, Jack's life was technically hers. He pointed at the gun. 'What are you going to do with that thing when we get there? Take it into the post office?'

'If I have to. Just get us there.'

'You don't even need me. You can give them your wife story.'

'Quicker if you flash your ID. I don't want to get into an argument with anybody, waste my time. Nobody speaks fucking English there anymore, either.'

'Look at the time, Larissa. Look at the traffic. It's not going to happen.'

'Just fucking drive.'

He drove. The world was all blurred wet light. It was difficult to see too far ahead. They crawled down Oxford Street.

Jack said: 'You don't seem too interested in Kim?'

'Why? Is she interesting?' Larissa's tone was firm and dismissive.

'Well, she's swiped a three-point-four-million-dollar treasure from under everybody's nose. I'd say that makes her pretty interesting.'

'Uh-huh.'

'That's it?'

'What do you want me to say? I've only met the bitch a couple of times. And now she's going to regret it.' She motioned with the gun. 'Drive faster.'

~35~

JACK SAW KIM FIRST. On the corner of York and Market streets, where the post office was situated in the arcade below street level. Shiny black raincoat, red tartan-patterned umbrella, red tartan-patterned miniskirt, black ankle boots. There was a package under her arm — and parked next to her, a medium-sized red wheelie suitcase with the arm extended up into the air. She was watching for a cab, but the only thing moving with any consistent pace in the city right now were umbrella-wielding pedestrians, and the monorail splashing everybody with more water from above.

Jack was on Market Street, in the middle lane. He glanced at Kim and said nothing. The lights turned green. The traffic moved up slowly.

'Can you see her?' asked Larissa, her voice tight with frustration.

'No.'

'We need to park somewhere.'

Jack was sweating, trying to keep an eye on Kim, and watching the brakelights flash on and off on the car in front, and willing the river of traffic to move, to pull them out of there and away down the hill. Larissa was turned to the driver's side, one leg bent and up on the seat, trying to see through the half-fogged windows. Ducking her head, looking around, left and right, up the street and down, desperate. She frowned at the rain and the blur and the *fucking* traffic. Then she put an arm on Jack's shoulder and leaned into him, hard.

'There she is! Quick, pull over!'

Jack looked at Larissa, hands on the steering wheel. The traffic going nowhere. She stuck the gun into his belly. 'Pull over, Jack.'

'I'm trying.'

The traffic surged forward about ten metres and then Jack was past the QVB, almost across from where he had seen Kim. Susko Books was just down on his left, at the end of York Street. Home. The traffic halted. Horns blared. He swung the BMW into the next lane and pulled up. More horns blared: then a taxi stopped right on his tail and flicked its hazard lights on and in the rear-view mirror Jack saw a couple of umbrellas lean in towards it. Larissa was yelling at him, desperate now, 'Come on! Let's go!', and she already had her leg out of the door, into the loud wet city, her Campers being rushed by the water in the gutter. Jack searched for Kim through the window, but could not see her anymore.

Larissa was out on the street now, looking over the roof, stepping up into the car with one foot and stretching for height, holding on to the edge of the open door, rain streaming over her and into the car. Then Jack heard a thud, a fist, or maybe the gun, hitting the roof. He was looking over at the corner, trying to see, taking snapshots in his mind with each gap in the traffic, searching for Kim with her tartan umbrella, straining through the sheeting rain and willing the stream of cowering pedestrians to get out of the way.

Then he saw. She was gone.

~36~

Larissa jumped back into the car and slammed the door.

'She got into a fucking cab! Come on, let's go. Airport.'

The lights changed on the intersection and a crossing button on a pole nearby started to tick, the sound padded and flatulent like a toy machine-gun, and people spilled onto the street, surrounding the BMW in a small sea of bank-logo umbrellas.

'Move, Jack!'

'You want me to run people over?'

The work-rush splashed on: nobody looked into the car as they walked past, nobody saw the beautiful girl with the gun in her hand. Everyday life streamed by. Heads were down, eyes trained on the puddles in the street.

Larissa was shaking her head, anger welling freely as she scowled at the people passing the car.

Jack had his hand on the door, ready to pop it and run.

'I'm going to kill that bitch.'

The lights changed. The last few pedestrians passed in front of the car.

'Go!'

Jack opened the door and jumped out of the Beamer.

Nobody shot him as he ran to the footpath.

He stood back from the road, under an awning, safe among his fellow citizens with takeaway coffee cups to their lips. He looked into the car. The windows were fogged up and streaked with rain and it was difficult to see inside. Three seconds later, the engine came to screeching life and the BMW sped off down the hill. A green light released more traffic behind it and the car disappeared into a river of flickering steel and light.

Jack stood there for a moment longer, getting himself together. As wet and wrung out as the day he was born.

~37~

THE ROUTE 389 BUS CRAWLED UP OXFORD STREET: packed, stuffed full of annoyed wet people and their dripping umbrellas. Jack had an aisle seat near the front. He sat and stared and felt his damp clothes stick uncomfortably to his body. Every now and then, a drop of water gathered at a hair tip and swelled and, after a small dramatic pause, spilled down the back of his neck or into his eyes. His head was really making him suffer. A man standing in the aisle bumped into his shoulder every time the bus lurched, which did not help the pain. And the woman sitting next to him would not stop talking into her mobile phone. She did not have much to say and what Jack heard could easily have been saved for later.

The bus stopped: more people squeezed on. Jack wondered what he would find back at De Groot Galleries. His head throbbed some more. His neighbour continued to complain into her mobile: '... Derek, he just doesn't get it, he's so insensitive, you know, and I really need him to be there for me right now ...' The guy standing in the aisle leaned his arse into him. The bus steamed.

He wondered if Kim had got onto a plane.

Back in Woollahra, the bus went along Moncur Street and then past Peaker Lane. Jack saw police cars and an ambulance choking the entrance and the ramp down to the car park under De Groot Galleries. Cops with raincoats and umbrellas all over the place. The bus pulled over at a stop right there and a couple of people got out and an old man and his hunched-over wife got on. It took them a while. Jack gave up his seat and moved down the aisle towards the back. As much as he wanted to leave the mobile sauna, for now he decided to stay put.

He was not worried about the cops so much: after all, Jack had not actually done anything. Neither had Kablunak, for that matter, if you did not count the original theft of the Sergius from wherever it had been stolen from. And Jack suspected that the Russian had probably called the cops on Rhonda himself — who else would have? — which was a sure sign that Kablunak had got out of the kitchen. Walter must have eventually wondered what the hell was going on and gone to look. But Jack had been the cause of quite a few of the more recent *hassles* that Viktor Kablunak had been forced to deal with; he had given up on ever seeing the Fleming book again, but was concerned now with any ideas the Russian might have for other types of retribution. His personality was a touch too *biblical* for Jack's liking. Plagues would not be out of the question with regards to Kablunak's vengeance.

Jack got out at Edgecliff station. Inside, he peeled a one-hundred-dollar bill off the wad in his pocket. He immediately felt a little better. He did not mind being wet so much. He went straight to a newsagent's and bought a packet of cigarettes. Camels. Then he jumped into a taxi and went home.

Jack had a shower, changed into some dry clothes and looked at the money. He smoked and counted it and fanned out the crisp one-hundred-dollar notes on the dining table and looked at it some more, then gathered it up and counted it again. He sipped from a nice bottle of twelve-year-old Bowmore single malt that he had treated himself to, and smoked more Camels with great pleasure. Lois scoffed down some top-shelf Norwegian sardines in the kitchen, straight from the can. Jack worried about her lips. He remembered what Kablunak had said to him. *Money has no soul. It is energy. It must move.*

Jack looked over at Lois. She was licking her chops clean. She glanced at him, just a hint of disdain in her eyes. *Do you get it yet, Jack?* she seemed to say. *Basically, it comes and it goes.*

The Russian appeared the next day. He found Jack walking down Oatley Road, on his way back home after buying more cigarettes. Cousin Carl was driving the car. He nodded at Jack through the window.

Kablunak was in the back. 'Need a lift, Mr Susko?'

In the Mercedes, Viktor Kablunak had selected *Ascenseur pour l'échafaud* by Miles Davis.

'Hey Carl,' said Jack as he slammed the door.

'Jack.'

Jack turned to Kablunak. 'New driver, huh?'

'Yes,' replied the Russian. 'Walter got a call-back. He is to be a singing policeman in a stage-musical. I am told the production will travel through regional New South Wales and Queensland. I believe this will be good for Walter, so I have given him two months' leave.'

'You're very kind.'

'Yes. I can be.'

Jack looked out through the window. Today, the sun was back out, heating the storm-soaked city like a giant jet engine, idling in the sky. Everything steamed and sweated. The streets were awash in drowned leaves, banked up and welded into the gutters. Birds chirped, drains gurgled. The people of Sydney walked around sluggish and sapped, flat as car batteries after a night with the lights left on. It was the perfect day for lying around and sweating and stroking your cat, for smoking cigarettes and eating pistachio nuts, and washing it all down with lots of quality Belgian beer — or maybe driving around with a jazz-loving Russian who may or may not want to hurt you.

'How's Pascal?'

'Recovering.'

'Oh, good,' said Jack. 'And Rhonda?'

'Cops got her,' said Carl.

'So what happened in the end?'

Viktor Kablunak grimaced. 'Please, Mr Susko. It is old

news and I have been repeating it all night with the police. So very boring, once it has happened, no?'

Jack tried to read between the lines, but it was all in Cyrillic.

'You look confused, Mr Susko.'

'It's just my head. Sometimes after intense gun-wielding adventures, I'm prone to suffer waves of nausea.'

'You must forget about it.'

They drove on. The sun had the girls out in skimpy clothes again. Jack wondered what Kim was wearing right now.

'I fear boredom far more than death, Mr Susko,' announced Viktor Kablunak, relaxed, very unlike a man who only yesterday had lost over three million dollars' worth of the Good Book. 'I have always sensed that you are of a similar attitude.'

'Who likes to be bored?'

'It is not a question of *like*. It is a question of the effort *not to be so*.'

'Right. I always thought it was a question of money.'

'Wrong. It is about *attitude*, Mr Susko.' Kablunak played along to the music on his thigh. 'Attitude and *intent*. Desire *enacted*. Action.' The Russian clapped his hands. 'Life with no consequence but death. Remember, Jack?'

'Who could forget?'

Kablunak's tone hardened. 'Do not dismiss this idea. I am still not sure what to do about you.'

'How about giving me my book back?'

'No.'

'Right,' said Jack. 'So we're okay, then?' His tone was bright, as though everything was nothing. He hoped

Kablunak would buy it.

No reply. They turned into Leinster Street. Kablunak still said nothing, stared out of the window at the hot bright day. A little further up, Carl pulled over. The Russian gestured to the door. Jack opened it and got out.

Through the open window, Viktor Kablunak said: 'You owe me, Mr Susko. I will let you know.'

~38~

THERE WAS SOMETHING IN THE WEEKEND PAPERS about it all. Rhonda Alexandra de Groot and Max Troy Martin were arrested and charged with the murders of Richard John de Groot and Lewis Hendrik Bloemsaat. Their trial was pending. Apparently, South African authorities were also keen to interview Mrs Rhonda de Groot over the theft of antique diamonds and some ancient tribal artefacts that her deceased husband was implicated in. Police refused to comment on the source of their tip-off.

Lois was out and about and Jack did not feel like being alone in the apartment. He went around to see Ray Campbell. Susko Books and the public hordes could wait another day. Maybe it was delayed shock that had him feeling strange? Or the return to nicotine? More likely, he just needed an afternoon full of margaritas.

Ray Campbell had stopped with the margaritas and was into Manhattans now. By the fourth one, Jack had told him all about it.

'And you never even got to see the Sergius?' Ray was almost beside himself.

'Just wasn't meant to be.' Jack dragged deeply on his cigarette. 'Only the five-buck paperback specials for Jack Susko.'

'But so close!'

'And yet …'

Ray sighed and shook his head. Hair slicked back, clean-shaven cheeks glowing with moisturiser and alcohol, he was dressed like some kind of Jay Gatsby: high-waisted, pleated grey pinstriped pants, white shirt with a paisley blue necktie, cufflinks, braces, and spats. The deckchair was gone and he was reclined in an old leather wingback. A worn but rare edition of Cornell Woolrich's 1927 novel, *Children of the Ritz*, was on the drinks stand beside him.

'To think whose hands have held it.' Ray reached across for the cocktail shaker and topped up his Manhattan. His was on the sweeter side and poured into a cocktail glass. No cherries because Ray never bought out of season. Jack preferred a four-to-one whiskey to vermouth in an old-fashioned lowball. He raised it to his lips, for a moment remembering Kim's hands on his shirt.

'So Kablunak called the cops?'

'Yep.' Jack tapped his cigarette into a chrome smoking-stand ashtray. 'They caught Rhonda and Max at the airport.'

'And what about the girls?'

'Gone.'

'Both of them?'

Jack nodded. 'Apparently.'

'My, my,' Ray sipped his Manhattan. He eyed Jack, gave a sympathetic smile. 'You liked this Kim, didn't you?' he said.

Jack weighed up his feelings as he stubbed out the cigarette. It was still too early to call. And what did it matter now, anyway?

He said: 'Maybe I was just about to, you know?'

~39~

Monday. Back to work. Somebody had left a box outside the front door of Susko Books. Whoever it was had written in thick black marker across the top: *All Yours!* Jack took it inside and dropped it on the counter. He lit a cigarette and had a look.

The Diamond in Your Pocket: Discovering Your True Radiance by Gangaji; *The Power of Vastu Living: Welcoming Your Soul into Your Home and Workplace* by Kathleen Cox; *Now Hear This Gentle Singing* by Meredith Mathers and Josephine Stone; *Meditation: the Complete Guide* by Patricia Monaghan and Eleanor G. Diereck; *The Silent Scream: Subconscious Trauma and How to Let It Out* by Helena le Brun and Gary Klein; *Life Is But a Dream … So Row!* by Reynold Knox; *After the Ecstasy, the Laundry* by Jack Kornfield; and *Knitted Animals* by Anne-Dorthe Grigaff.

Everything you needed to read to get your shit together. Maybe Jack would take the afternoon off and have a little flip-through.

The phone started ringing. He tossed *Knitted Animals* back into the box, came around the counter and picked up.

'Susko Books.'

'Where the fuck's my car?'

Chester Sinclair. *Shit*. Jack had still not been out to pick up the Fiori. 'What's the author's name?'

'What?' There was a pause as Sinclair thought about it. 'Don't give me any of your crap, Susko! Where's my car?'

'Being serviced as we speak,' said Jack, surprised at how smooth he managed to sound. He went with it. 'Then I've got it booked in for a Super Clean Supreme at *Super-Clean-All-Hand-Wash*. As a sign of my appreciation.'

'You're fucking with me.'

'Chester, you won't recognise it.'

Pause. 'Okay. What about Babylon Boy? You made the bet, right?'

This time Jack was not as quick off the cuff. He said, 'Um ...' and Chester was all over him.

'Oh don't fucking say it! You made the bet, didn't you, Jack? Tell me you made the fucking bet!'

'Sorry, Chester. Just couldn't get there on time.'

Silence. He could sense Sinclair's rage down the line. He heard a throat being cleared.

'Jack,' said Chester, voice calm but wound tight. 'Babylon Boy fucking *romped* it home, just like Eddie Roy said it would. Do you understand?' He cleared his throat again.

'Now, according to my calculations, the fifty dollars you were kindly asked to place on that horse in that race would have returned winnings of' — Jack heard paper rustling — 'six hundred and twenty-two dollars and ten cents. See what I'm getting at, Jack?'

'Loud and clear.'

'Don't make me call the cops.'

'I'll bring the car and the money round tonight. Okay?'

'Just don't make me call the cops.'

Chester Sinclair hung up.

After the rent — home and business — the credit cards, the overdrafts, the outstanding invoices, the backed-up phone and gas and electricity bills, and goddamn Chester with his car and his horse, Jack's ten-thousand-dollar money fan was significantly reduced in size. He managed to buy himself a couple of things: some vinyl, some CDs, some new clothes and a haircut. He managed to toss a few gold coins into a few homeless cups and hands around the city. He even managed to stock up on booze and cigarettes, going for the middle ground in quality, so that it might stretch a little further into the New Year. And then that was pretty much it. Which was great. Because everything was only up to Jack's neck again. He was used to it there. And at least he could breathe.

Two weeks later, an airmail envelope arrived in the post. From Paris. No return address. Jack tore it open with a blue Bic and pulled out what was inside. British Airways airline ticket. And a note.

Hi Jack

Paris is unbelievable!
Why don't you come over?

Kim xox

Jack read the note again. Then he put it and the plane ticket down on the counter and lit a cigarette. He smoked and stared out into the quiet shelves of Susko Books. He was trying to remember if he and Lois still had valid passports.